P9-CEU-962

UNDER THE GUN

The man with the shotgun missed, but the blast was loud enough to stagger Clint back as his ears erupted with a piercing shriek.

Clint stood in the middle of the crowd of gunmen. There were more of them dead or wounded at his feet than there were still shooting, but the ringing in his ears was enough to keep him from hearing anything else—and he was disoriented enough to feel his balance wavering as well. The man who'd just fired still had one barrel loaded and ready in the shotgun. Standing close enough to see the whites of the shotgunner's eyes, Clint knew he didn't stand much of a chance.

There was nobody standing between him and the shotgun, and the other man's finger was tightening on the trigger. . . .

DON'T MISS THESE
ALL-ACTION WESTERN SERIES
FROM THE BERKLEY PUBLISHING GROUP

THE GUNSMITH by J. R. Roberts
Clint Adams was a legend among lawmen, outlaws, and ladies. They called him . . . the Gunsmith.

LONGARM by Tabor Evans
The popular long-running series about Deputy U.S. Marshal Long—his life, his loves, his fight for justice.

SLOCUM by Jake Logan
Today's longest-running action Western. John Slocum rides a deadly trail of hot blood and cold steel.

BUSHWHACKERS by B. J. Lanagan
An action-packed series by the creators of Longarm! The rousing adventures of the most brutal gang of cutthroats ever assembled—Quantrill's Raiders.

DIAMONDBACK by Guy Brewer
Dex Yancey is Diamondback, a Southern gentleman turned con man when his brother cheats him out of the family fortune. Ladies love him. Gamblers hate him. But nobody pulls one over on Dex. . . .

WILDGUN by Jack Hanson
The blazing adventures of mountain man Will Barlow—from the creators of Longarm!

TEXAS TRACKER by Tom Calhoun
Meet J. T. Law: the most relentless—and dangerous—man-hunter in all Texas. Where sheriffs and posses fail, he's the best man to bring in the most vicious outlaws—for a price.

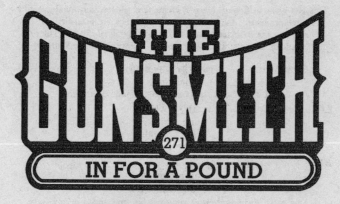

THE GUNSMITH

271

IN FOR A POUND

J. R. ROBERTS

JOVE BOOKS, NEW YORK

If you purchased this book without a cover, you should be aware that this book is stolen property. It was reported as "unsold and destroyed" to the publisher, and neither the author nor the publisher has received any payment for this "stripped book."

This is a work of fiction. Names, characters, places, and incidents either are the product of the author's imagination or are used fictitiously, and any resemblance to actual persons living or dead, business establishments, events, or locales is entirely coincidental.

IN FOR A POUND

A Jove Book / published by arrangement with
the author

PRINTING HISTORY
Jove edition / July 2004

Copyright © 2004 by Penguin Group (USA) Inc.

All rights reserved.
This book, or parts thereof, may not be reproduced in any form without permission. The scanning, uploading, and distribution of this book via the Internet or via any other means without the permission of the publisher is illegal and punishable by law. Please purchase only authorized electronic editions, and do not participate in or encourage electronic piracy of copyrighted materials. Your support of the author's rights is appreciated.
For information address: The Berkley Publishing Group,
a division of Penguin Group (USA) Inc.,
375 Hudson Street, New York, New York 10014.

ISBN: 0-515-13775-8

A JOVE BOOK®
Jove Books are published by The Berkley Publishing Group,
a division of Penguin Group (USA) Inc.,
375 Hudson Street, New York, New York 10014.
JOVE and the "J" design
are trademarks belonging to Penguin Group (USA) Inc.

PRINTED IN THE UNITED STATES OF AMERICA

10 9 8 7 6 5 4 3 2 1

ONE

"No good deed goes unpunished." Jack Bates lifted his glass to that and smiled proudly as though he were the one to bring that saying to life. When he looked over, he found the other man at his table lifting his glass as well.

"Who said that?" Clint asked after taking a sip of his beer. "Benjamin Franklin?"

Jack shrugged. "I don't know. Probably. But it's still true today as whenever it was said the first time and don't you forget it."

So far that evening, Jack had put away two or three drinks to every one of Clint's. Because of that, Clint wasn't too surprised that the other man was starting to ramble on a bit. "What brought on that little observation?"

Jack looked around at his surroundings. They were seated in a large saloon facing a stage full of dancing girls kicking up their heels to the tunes of a fairly talented piano player. It wasn't the best show in the country, but still better than most. The girls were pretty and scantily dressed and their routine was just lively enough to keep their skirts flying well above their knees.

The saloon itself was one of the newer ones in the area. So much so that the place still smelled like freshly cut lumber. Being a new place with a good show, the saloon was full of patrons in all stages of drunkenness. Despite all the smiles around him, however, Jack couldn't quite seem to find his own.

"Not sure," Jack finally said in answer to Clint's question. "Guess I was just thinking is all."

Clint smirked and gave the other man a pat on the shoulder. "Well, don't think too hard, Jack. You might sprain something."

Jack was a solidly built man with light brown hair and a barrel chest. He was the type of man that seemed to fill up more than his share of space not only because of his bulk, but because of his normally boisterous personality. That personality shone through as he slapped his hand against the table and lifted his glass one more time.

"See there? Now that's just why I wanted you here with me, Clint. I need someone to talk sense to me instead of just bending my ear. Here's to ya!"

As he drank a good portion of the beer that was remaining in his glass, Clint noticed Jack tipping his head back all the way so he could pour every last drop down his throat. When Jack put his glass down, he did so with enough force to almost tip the table off its legs.

"Damn, it sure is good to have you here, Clint! You're a sight for sore eyes!"

"So you mentioned." Actually, Clint figured he'd gotten that particular comment from the other man at least a dozen times by now.

Since he was always traveling from one place to another, Clint made a habit of checking in with his friend Rick Hartman in west Texas every now and then. Rick owned a saloon down there which was one of the few places in the country that Clint considered a home. Plenty of other folks knew about Clint's connection to the place and tended to look for him there since it was hard to tell where else he could be.

When Clint had checked in via telegraph with Rick, his friend let him know that he had a message waiting for him from another acquaintance in Nevada by the name of Jack Bates. Since Clint was in the area and hadn't looked in on Jack for some time, he decided to reply to the message in person. To say that Jack had been happy to see him would have been an understatement.

The last time Clint had been through that particular corner of Nevada, Driver's Town hadn't even been there. The town was so new that none of the buildings had gotten a chance to spring leaks yet and the ruts in the streets were hardly more than shallow grooves. Businesses were being started and homes were being built, all in a way that reminded Clint of what had made this country what it was: folks trying their best to build something.

Clint felt the excitement in the air when he'd first ridden into town and could still feel it in the crowded saloon. Actually, in the company of Jack Bates, he could feel the anticipation like something crackling through the clouds just before a storm. Jack always had a way of throwing himself into whatever project he'd decided to tackle and this was no exception.

"So when are you going to show me what made you write that letter to drag me all the way over here?" Clint asked. "Or was that just a bunch of smoke to pull me into one of your famous poker games?"

"It wasn't smoke, my friend," Jack said, then added with a wink and nudge of his elbow, "Well, no more than usual, anyway. Tell you the truth, I didn't expect you to show up in town so soon. I sent that letter less than a month ago."

"And some folks consider punctuality a good thing."

"Oh, don't get cross. You know what I mean. I can take you out to see my baby, but it might be better when there's more light."

"It's not too dark just yet. Besides, I think you could

use some fresh air after all that liquor you've been knocking back."

Jack squawked loudly and pushed away from the table. When he got to his feet, there was a bit of unsteadiness, but not enough to take him off his balance. "I can hold my own, thank you very much. And if you want to see my baby, then by all means, let's go see her. Lord knows I never get tired of the sight."

Clint got up from his chair and polished off the last of his beer. Like most saloons just starting out, the drinks were strong and the girls were all smiles. Nothing like putting the best foot forward, especially for a business that thrived on high spirits.

Navigating their way through the crowd to the front door was no easy task. As the sun dropped farther below the horizon, more and more bodies seemed to find their way to the saloon and the opening week specials being offered inside. Jack led the way, taking his time to shake hands and wave to any and every face that was turned in, his direction. Clint just kept moving along, wanting to get outside before it truly was too late to see anything.

Nevada's nights had a special kind of darkness all their own. On one hand, the skies were wide open and filled with so many stars that it resembled a river bottom after a spill of diamonds. The moon gave off a silvery glow as well, which added to the cool luminescence washing down from above. On the other hand, even with the stars and moon overhead, the shadows seemed blacker and the darkness seemed twice as thick as other places.

Perhaps it was the desert nearby that made the night seem especially formidable. Whatever it was, Clint found that the light just seemed to get sucked out of the air in that part of the country. Luckily, by the time he and Jack made it out of the saloon, there was still enough of the dusk lingering in the skies to fight back the approaching shadows.

"This way," Jack said, turning to walk down the street toward the edge of town. "Of course, there ain't much to see just yet, but before you know it, I'll have enough built up to knock yer socks off."

"Just mine?" Clint asked.

"Well, you or anyone else that's got the good sense to invest. But not too many more. I can't cut the pie into too many pieces or I won't be able to taste it for myself."

"How many others have you contacted?"

"A few. Not many have taken me up on the offer, though."

They were already almost to the town's border. Clint rolled his eyes at Jack's evasive answer, but knew better than to expect much more. Besides, he wanted to get a look at what had gotten Jack's feathers so ruffled before pressing the matter any further. Judging by the way Jack came to a stop a minute or so later and spread out his arms, Clint wasn't going to have to wait any longer.

"Here it is, Clint. Feast your eyes on it!"

Even in the fading light of dusk, it was plain to see that there wasn't much behind Jack apart from a stretch of open land and the skeletal beginnings of a structure that was only partially completed. Despite that fact, Jack motioned toward those unimpressive things as if they were standing on the edge of the Promised Land.

Grinning proudly, Jack announced, "The Grand Bates Raceway!"

TWO

Clint nodded and slowly took another look at what he was being shown. It didn't take more than another couple of seconds for him to get his fill of the sight. After that, he turned his gaze over to Jack who was still standing there like a proud pappa.

"The Grand Bates Raceway?" Clint asked.

"Either that or the Bates Grand Raceway. I haven't decided yet."

"This is the business venture you mentioned in your letter? A racetrack?"

"Of course it is. What did you think it would be, Clint?"

"All you said was a sporting venue and an attraction to bring in people from neighboring towns and states alike." Clint was quoting most of that from the exact text of the letter that Rick had telegraphed to him. Upon saying them, the words seemed even more showy than when he'd read them.

Jack, on the other hand, reacted as though he was listening to a simple grocery list. "Yeah. That sounds about right. So what else did you think it would be?"

"A saloon. A gambling hall. Hell, it could have been a cathouse for all I know!"

"But this is so much better!"

"A racetrack," Clint said, just to make sure he wasn't hearing something wrong.

Jack turned around so he could look at the open land and partially completed structure himself. "Yes, siree. A racetrack. And a damn fine one once she's all put together."

"Isn't this town a bit small for a racetrack?"

"Right now it is, sure. But that only means I can get the land for a song. I was even able to talk to some of the other forward-thinking businessmen around here and get them to throw their hats into the ring as well. After all, a racetrack can bring a lot of attention to this place and that means only one thing: expansion. The way I see it, this could be as big as San Francisco in no time at all."

Even though he was looking at nothing more than a pile of wooden studs on a plot of land, Clint had no problem believing that Jack had committed himself to a dream as big as the one he was describing. In fact, that tendency to dream was part of the reason he'd answered Jack's letter. The only problem was that he'd hoped to arrive before Jack could commit too much of himself to another expensive venture.

No matter how close he'd been when he'd gotten the message or how fast he'd ridden into Driver's Town, Clint was still too late to accomplish that first goal.

Deciding it was better to go along with Jack for the moment instead of trying to buck the other man's optimistic tide, Clint said, "All right then. Let's get a look at this grand raceway of yours."

"Well, it'd be better to save the big tour for tomorrow when it's light out, but you can see a good portion of it now. That's the track over there," he said, pointing toward the open stretch of land. "And those," Jack added, motioning to the partially completed structure, "are the stands. The stables will be built right next to them."

Clint squinted into the darkness and picked out a smaller shape moving beyond the structure onto the track. "Looks like we're not the only ones out for a tour this evening."

"What do you mean?" Jack asked. The moment his eyes fixed on the shape that Clint had spotted, Jack was off and running. All the while, he grumbled loudly to himself about trespassers and the various ugly things he'd like to do once he got his hands on them.

Clint followed along as well as his mind raced to come up with a way to figure just how far into the hole Jack had already gotten himself.

The farther he walked, the closer Clint got to the seats that were being built near the track. And the closer he got, the bigger they seemed. Another thing he quickly noticed was that there didn't seem to be much else around the base of the building except for the beginnings of a staircase leading up to the ascending levels.

Normally, something under construction had things lying close by like tools or piles of lumber. From what Clint could see, either the men working on the stands were especially tidy at the end of every day or they hadn't been working on the site at all for some time.

For his part, Jack seemed more concerned with a single trespasser. "Hey!" he shouted. "You there! This is private property."

The figure in the darkness stopped right where it was with one foot on the land that had been cleared off for the track. From there, the person pivoted around to look at Clint and Jack, waiting patiently for both men to arrive.

It didn't matter how dark it was, there was no possible way that Clint could have missed the fact that the trespasser was a woman. He would have had to have been blind not to see the woman's shapely figure and thick, flowing hair. As a matter of fact, the pale light from the moon and stars seemed to accentuate the curves of her body until Clint nearly stopped in his own tracks.

Jack might have been worked up, but he noticed the woman's figure as well. When he did, he propped his hands upon his hips and spoke in a bellowing voice. "Laura! Is that you?"

The woman put her hands on her own hips as if to mock the way Jack was staring at her. "If you wouldn't drink so damn much every other night, you might not get so wound up for no reason. Yeah, it's me!"

Laughing and rubbing his eyes, Jack turned around to look at Clint who was just walking up beside him. "Clint Adams, this is Laura Damon. Laura, this is Clint Adams."

As the woman walked closer, she seemed to get even more attractive. Dressed in battered jeans and a man's shirt that was tied at her stomach, she was making no effort to hide the impressive figure that had caught Clint's eye. By the look on her face, it was easy to tell that Laura wasn't too displeased by what she was seeing either.

"Nice to meet you, Clint," she said after he'd taken her hand. "I'm Jack's partner."

THREE

When Clint shook Laura's hand, he found her to have a strength that lay right beneath her surface. Although she didn't try to grip his hand too tightly, she let him know that she was far from delicate by giving him a confident grip and looking directly into his eyes as she spoke.

"Clint Adams? Really?" she asked.

"Well, sure," Jack answered. "Who else? Didn't I tell you he was coming?"

"You say a lot of things, Jack. I can't exactly set my watch to every last one of them."

Clint smirked at the exchange. "So I see that you truly do know Jack fairly well. How long have you been partners?"

"Ever since he talked me into sinking my money into this racetrack idea of his. It's been a few months now, but it feels like a hell of a lot longer than that sometimes."

"Oh, hush up, girl," Jack scolded. "Let me and Mr. Adams here walk the property in peace."

Clint fell into step with Jack on one side and Laura on the other. He paid attention to about half of what Jack was saying since most of it was colorful embellishments about what the racetrack would be once it was completed. The rest of his attention was focused on Laura, who walked beside him and appeared to be blocking out Jack's ongoing diatribe as well.

The dusk had faded completely away, leaving only the stars and a piece of the moon to illuminate the night. That pale light flowed like cream over the skin of Laura's face, neck and arms. But rather than soak into her, it seemed to roll over her every curve. There was a gentle bounce in her steps that caused her breasts to sway beneath her shirt. The chill in the air had already caused her nipples to harden and poke slightly at the coarse material covering them.

Neither she nor Clint said a word as they walked. Instead, they quietly examined each other as Jack pointed here and there, giving a bloated story to every corner of the track. Even in the darkness, Clint could tell that Laura's skin was richly tanned and smooth. Her lips were full and curled into a welcoming smile that was reflected in her eyes.

Having come to the end of his most recent sales pitch, Jack stopped and spun around to face his partner and his friend. "So what were you doing out here all alone anyway, Laura?"

The mention of her name snapped her attention away from Clint and she responded as though the answer had already been locked and loaded. "I come out here a lot to walk and clear my head. Used to be that I would check up on the builders' progress."

"Yeah," Jack said, glancing back to the uncompleted structure nearby. "Guess there's no reason for that lately."

Clint didn't have to look back to see that the stands still hadn't completed themselves. "Then I'm right to think that whoever was building back there isn't doing so anymore."

Jack's hands were stuffed into his pockets and he ground his boot against the dirt. "Yeah. You're right to think that."

"Kind of hard to tell in this light," Clint said, "but it seems like there hasn't been anyone working on those stands for a good long while."

"Not that long."

"A month, actually," Laura put in. When she saw Jack look up at her with a glare, she added, "It's been a month today. That's part of the reason why I needed to walk around and clear my head. My life's savings keeps getting farther and farther out of my reach."

With that, the entire area seemed to become dead quiet. Jack was staring down at his feet, unable to come up with any kind of response to what Laura had said. Jack was dressed in a suit that had become rumpled during the night in the saloon, but at that moment he looked like a small boy who'd been called out for a wrong he'd done.

For a moment, Clint thought that he sensed a genuine regret in Jack's expression. In all the times he'd seen him and throughout all the schemes Jack had concocted, Clint really hadn't seen Jack regret a single one of them. Suddenly that trace of regret disappeared, leaving Jack looking just as Clint always remembered him.

"It's just a minor setback," the other man said brightly. "I told you that a while ago and now that Clint's here, we can get right back on track."

"Hold on there," Clint said, stopping as though he was about to physically walk over a line in the dirt. "I've only been in town a few hours and we haven't talked about much more than old times and the next round of drinks."

Jack shrugged and said, "I know. I didn't think we'd worry about business until—"

"Until what? You made me another one of your partners?"

Laura had to smirk at that one. It seemed that Clint was very familiar with the way Jack liked to work with people.

The expression on Jack's face was a theatrical mix of sadness and emotional pain. "Clint, that hurts."

"Yeah, yeah. I'll bet it wounds you to the core. Now how about you fill me in on what the hell is going on here, why you wanted me to come out here and what you expect me to do about this racetrack of yours?"

Cautious as to what he wanted to say next, Jack bought himself some time by looking over to Laura and holding out his hands imploringly. Mercifully enough, she stepped in to aid her partner.

"Actually," she said, "this isn't all his fault. I've been in on a few other prospects with Jack and a lot of them turn out to be . . . well . . . less than what he made them out to be."

"That's not—" Jack started to say, but was cut off by a swiftly raised hand from both Clint and Laura. After that, he piped down and let her go on.

"This racetrack was scheduled to go on as planned and actually looked like it might pan out. The builders were here, ahead of schedule, and everything was going along fine."

"Then what happened?" Clint asked, knowing another boot had to drop sooner or later.

Laura took a deep breath and replied, "Then I found out that Jack wasn't exactly the first person to get the idea to build a racetrack in this area."

"Is that a fact?" As Clint asked that question, he turned his gaze over toward Jack, who was still fidgeting from one foot to another.

Jack pretended to ignore the eyes that were upon him, but couldn't hold out for more than a few seconds before cracking. "Nobody else thought about having a racetrack here! Everyone says Driver's Town is too small for it."

"And where were you when you got this brainstorm of yours?" Clint asked.

"I can answer that," came a voice from the vicinity of the uncompleted rows of seats.

Clint had heard steps coming from that direction moments ago. Being in the wide-open land where the proposed track was to be, there wasn't much to keep every little sound from reaching his ears. He couldn't be sure if the figures were just walking by or if they were going to stop. Apparently, it was the latter.

Keeping the new arrivals in the corner of his eye, Clint watched for Jack's and Laura's reactions to tell him who those others might be. Laura seemed to be surprised at the sound of the voices. Jack, on the other hand, looked as if someone had just walked over his grave.

FOUR

There were three of them in all. Three figures stepped out from where they'd been hidden behind the awkward structure of the stands. Although the construction was far from being completed, there were enough struts in place to hide other people besides the three men they could see at the moment.

Having gotten what he needed from Jack's expression, Clint turned to face the approaching strangers. "You know these guys, don't you Jack?"

It was more of a statement than a question and Jack responded grudgingly.

"I got a good idea who they could be."

The first of the men walked a few steps ahead of the other two. He had a medium build and carried himself like he thought he was twice the size. That was probably because of the other two men behind him who were put together like brick walls.

"Forget who we are," that first man said. "I'm more concerned about the two people you have with you, Jack. I heard you had a lady working with you, but . . ." He let his words trail off as he started to drink in the sight of Laura in a long, lingering stare. "Mmm. I didn't think

15

you'd have a lady as tasty looking as that in on this. And you," he said, switching his stare over toward Clint, "I don't think we've had the pleasure."

"No," Clint said before Jack had a chance to say anything. "We haven't. Perhaps you'd like to introduce yourselves."

"I could. Or maybe Jack would like to do that for me."

The trio had come to a stop several paces in front of Clint, Laura and Jack. Even in the dim light of the stars, it was plain to see that all three men were armed. The pale light of the moon glanced off of the pistol handles hanging at each of the strangers' sides and illuminated the cocky smiles on their faces as well.

"I was just about to tell you about these fellas," Jack said. "They're probably working for a man who thinks he's the only one with the right to build anything in the state of Nevada."

"Aw, that's not the case," the spokesman for the strangers said. "But my employer did have the notion to build a racetrack before you did. In fact, some might say you stole that idea right out from under him. That's not a very sporting thing to do."

"No," Clint said. "It sure isn't."

The spokesman rocked back on his heels and took a slow look around him. "Well, I don't think any of you folks should worry about anything. Since it seems that this racetrack isn't going to be anything but a plot of empty land and half a building, I'd say our account is settled."

It wasn't Clint who spoke out next. It wasn't even Jack. Laura's voice cut through the night with an edge of its own.

"You three don't have the right to tell anyone what to do," she said. "And neither does your employer. Folks can build whatever they want if they have the means and they can't be stopped just because someone's afraid of a little competition."

Both of the hulking men behind the spokesman bristled at that and their hands drifted toward the guns at their sides. The spokesman held out his arms to keep them back, but he didn't seem any less angry. "Oh, the problem here ain't competition. It's about some people not doing what they were told back when it was told to them politely. Jack had the chance to go in on a racetrack and passed it up. Ain't that right, Jack?"

Jack gritted his teeth, but didn't say a word in response to the question posed to him.

That didn't seem to bother the spokesman one bit. "But rather than take the deal he was offered, he went on by hisself and broke ground on his own track. There don't need to be two tracks in these parts, Jack. I'm saving you a whole lot of money and trouble by getting you to stop before getting run out of business later down the road."

"And maybe it'll be us running you out of business," Laura offered. "I'll bet that's the real reason you came all this way."

Clint didn't know exactly who the other three men were or who they represented. It didn't take much of a thinker to put together what they were after, however, and now wasn't the time to figure out the rest. "All right," he said. "It looks to me like you boys already got what you wanted. Nothing's being put together right now or anytime real soon, so how about you three just save the rest of your tough talk and call it a night?"

"Well, there's where you made a mistake, mister," the spokesman said. "I'm pretty happy with what I see so far, but that's not the only reason we came."

Already, one of the bigger thugs with the spokesman had turned and started walking toward the unfinished stands. It was at that moment that Clint spotted something in the distance that he hadn't seen before.

"A man like Jack ain't destined for nothing but failure anyhow, but I'm supposed to make sure of that firsthand," the spokesman pointed out. "And more than that, I'm supposed to make sure that he don't pick up where he left off anytime soon."

Jack stepped forward and watched as the man nearing the stands walked toward the distant shapes that Clint had spotted. Those shapes were slightly smaller than tree stumps and topped with small, bent handles as well as little spouts on their sides.

Clint wasn't sure what those other shapes were until the big man walked up to them and picked them up. The sloshing sound washed through the air like water lapping against a pier. A couple seconds after the big man dumped some of the contents of the container onto the lowest row of the stands, the scent of kerosene drifted into Clint's nostrils.

"Hey!" Jack said once he picked up the scent as well. "Stop that!"

The spokesman and the other ox behind him slapped their hands against their guns and positioned themselves between the track and the stands.

"Best hold it right there, Jack," the spokesman warned. "Or you'll get a real close look at this fire."

FIVE

Until now, Clint had been hoping to let the situation pass without violence. Until now, he'd thought he'd just see what was going on and act on it once the storm had passed. But that storm had suddenly become the kind that threatened not just one structure but the entire town if the wind picked up just right.

Before Clint could say another word against what was about to happen, Jack stepped forward as though he didn't even see the guns the other men were carrying. "That is enough!" Jack shouted. "I won't have you burn down my racetrack before it even gets finished."

Jack wasn't the only one to protest. Even Laura was moving toward the spokesman and his hulking guard with fire in her eyes. "I'll get Sheriff Meeks down here right now and he'll see to it that—"

"That what?" the spokesman interrupted. "That he scoops up your dead bodies? 'Cause that's all that'll be left if you take one more step."

Jack didn't move, although every muscle in his body was twitching to bring him closer to those stands.

Laura was frozen in her tracks, fear mixed with anger on her face.

It was Clint who moved. He was careful not to do anything too suddenly, but he also knew he couldn't just stand by and let the big man with the kerosene light the match he'd just dug from his pocket.

Clint took a cautious step forward holding both hands in front of him. "This can't—" was all he got out before the spokesman tightened his grip around his pistol and drew it out from its holster.

After that, there were no more words to be said.

The big man closest to the spokesman had his gun already halfway drawn, so he was the first of those two to clear leather. His meaty hand enveloped the pistol and brought it up quickly, if a bit clumsily.

Clint saw that gun as the most immediate threat, so he shifted his aim toward the big man. His mind and body acted as one. The moment he picked his target, his arm moved to comply. The modified Colt was pointed like one of Clint's own fingers and a heartbeat later the hammer dropped.

Sparks and smoke spewed from the gun's barrel and a chunk of lead spat through the air. The Colt bucked against Clint's palm, but he had already shifted it toward its next target.

The spokesman was dropping to one knee to get off a shot when the round from Clint's gun whipped through the air and punched a messy hole into the big man behind him. Bending his gun arm at the elbow, the spokesman aimed from the hip and squeezed off a shot.

Things were moving too quickly for the spokesman to know who exactly had fired that first gunshot, so he just aimed at all three of his adversaries. Even with the blood pounding through his veins, the trio wasn't too easy to miss.

•   •   •

Clint's eyes had picked out the gun in the spokesman's hand a second before it was fired. Reacting instinctively, he reached out with his free hand to grab hold of the closest person he could reach and throw out of the way of the incoming fire. There was no way Clint could know exactly where the other man was aiming, but he was thinking clearly enough to make a good guess.

The last time he'd checked on her, Laura had been behind Clint and a bit to one side. Now Clint could see that she wasn't about to take the burning of her stands lightly; she had already started running toward the man with the kerosene when the shooting had started. That meant Jack was the one in Clint's reach, so Jack was the one who was pulled right off his feet and tossed unceremoniously to the ground.

"What the—?" Jack sputtered before the wind was knocked out of him.

"Shut up and stay there," Clint snarled. Not wanting to waste any more time, he fired a shot at the spokesman and started moving toward Laura.

In the time that they'd been talking, Clint hadn't spotted any weapon on Laura whatsoever. He knew that she must have been hiding one on her somewhere because she now had it drawn and was taking shots at the man with the kerosene while walking fearlessly toward the stands.

"Get the hell away from there!" she screamed as she squeezed her trigger.

Clint winced as her gun went off and sent a shot toward the wood that had been doused with kerosene. He was about five or six feet from her back by this point and he covered the rest of the distance with a mighty jump that brought him close enough to wrap one arm around Laura's waist so she could be taken down along with him as he fell.

Tensing in his grasp and twisting around to see who

had taken hold of her, Laura muttered a few confused curses as she was overcome by Clint's weight.

More shots rang through the air, most of which were not being fired at Clint or Laura. The spokesman had managed to squeeze his trigger and the man with the kerosene was just taking aim with his own pistol. The rest of the shots were coming from the vicinity of the track, which meant that Jack must have had a gun on him as well.

"Great," Clint grunted as he pressed Laura down closer to the ground while thinking about all the firearms coming to bear. "This is just great."

The only thing in Clint's favor was that apparently none of the other people around him were expert marksmen. So far, it appeared as if the only one seriously hurt was the big man that Clint had put down himself. Of course, that didn't mean that the others weren't still going to fill the air with as much lead as they could.

That, alone, made every last one of them dangerous.

The spokesman took another shot and moments after his gun went off, he recoiled as a piece of hot lead chewed through his shoulder. He cursed loudly and tried to focus so he could return fire, but was knocked flat onto his back by a bullet from Clint's modified Colt.

Looking back, Clint shouted to the man who'd put the shot through the spokesman's shoulder. "Jack, for Christ's sake, get down!"

Too excited after having scored a hit on his target, Jack barely noticed that Clint was talking to him. The words coming out of Clint's mouth didn't even come close to registering in his racing mind.

Clint had been in enough firefights to recognize the look of excited fear in Jack's eyes. Short of dropping him with a round from his own gun, Clint knew that Jack was too worked up to listen to reason at that particular moment. That just meant more direct methods would be necessary.

Unfortunately, it didn't look like Clint would have much time to use those methods.

"What the hell are you waiting for?" the spokesman cried painfully from his spot on the ground. "Light it!"

Hearing that was all Jack needed to forget about whatever doubts might have been going through his mind. Of course, common sense went out the window right along with his fears and doubts as he started running straight toward the stands. His path took him right into the waiting sights of the two remaining gunmen.

The man with the kerosene had a gun in one hand and a match in the other. With a flick of his wrist, he struck the match against his belt buckle while taking aim with his pistol. A nasty smile curled his lips up over his teeth.

SIX

Clint's gun was half empty.

The people around him were either trying to shoot him or were running headlong into the oncoming fire. And the only shelter in his line of sight was seconds away from going up in flames.

It wasn't the worst night of his life, but it was getting there fast.

Springing to his feet, he pushed Laura down hard enough so that she wouldn't be right behind him. He threw himself into a run the moment both boots were beneath him and he lifted the Colt to take his next shot.

The spokesman was down, but not out, and he was lifting his gun in a shaking hand to take a shot at Jack. All the shakes in the world would have had to take over that man's hand for him to miss Jack, who was less than a foot or two in front of him.

What made it bad for Clint was that Jack had also positioned himself so that he was blocking a clear shot at the spokesman. Rather than waste time he didn't have, Clint played the cards he'd been dealt and took the only real shot available to him.

Jack was running at full speed toward the gunman with

the match. His eyes were wild, and he hadn't been able to hit much of anything even though he was armed and eager to fire.

With all that in mind, Clint took a fraction of a second to aim and then squeezed his trigger. The Colt barked once and sent its round into the night where it hit its mark perfectly. The bullet nipped at the side of Jack's leg, barely glancing off of bone before continuing on. The damage was minimal, but the impact of the lead against his leg was the next best thing to Clint being there to kick the other man's feet out from under him.

Jack went down almost instantly. His face pinched in from the bite of pain in his leg and his arms swung out to either side in an attempt to catch himself as he fell. His gun went off, but it was only because his hands had clenched shut out of sheer reflex.

Half a heartbeat after Jack fell down, the spokesman took a shot of his own. If Jack had still been running at him, the spokesman's shot would have landed square in Jack's chest. As it was, the bullet hissed through empty air, along with another shot fired by the man with the kerosene.

With Jack down for the moment, Clint started running as fast as he could toward the stands. Along the way, he ran by the spokesman and laid that one out with a blow to the back of his head using the butt of his modified Colt. The spokesman got out half a curse before he slumped over with blood trickling from the wound above his hairline.

That only left the man with the kerosene in Clint's sights. Although he hadn't hit Jack with the shot he'd taken, the man by the stands didn't seem too concerned. Instead, his focus was on the match in his other hand, which he prepared to flick toward the oil-soaked side of the stands.

As he ran, Clint read the intentions of the man in front

of him the way other people might read a newspaper. He watched the motion of the man's arms and the shift of his eyes, all of which stood out to him even in the dim light of the stars.

Clint lifted his Colt and prepared to fire, knowing that the number of live rounds in his cylinder was getting dangerously low. Before he could shoot, he saw the other man's hand twitch as the match leaped outward toward the kerosene. Clint readjusted his aim as he ran another step, let out his breath and fired.

The Colt barked once and bucked in his hand. The bullet spun from its cylinder, through the barrel, across several feet of open air and then finally clipped the top of the matchstick a few inches before flame touched kerosene.

The matchstick jerked awkwardly in midair and seemed to hang there for a second. All that came from its tip was a few jagged splinters and a wisp of smoke. Momentum carried the matchstick the rest of the way to the structure, but the splinter of wood merely slapped against its wet surface.

Clint had one bullet left. He'd saved it just in case the man with the kerosene had decided to test his luck even after all he'd seen. Still running toward the stands, Clint would have been more than happy to finish the confrontation without another raised hand or unkind word.

There wasn't going to be a fire and that caused Clint to breathe much easier.

"Think about this for a moment," Clint said as he came to a stop less than four feet from the other man. "It's already over. You can walk out of here or be carried away. The choice is yours."

The man with the kerosene still held his gun. He had more shots than Clint and plenty more matches in his pocket. He even had the physical advantage, since he easily outweighed Clint by at least a hundred pounds of muscle.

Knowing all of that well enough, the other man still didn't seem to be in any hurry to act. In fact, his eyes glanced over Clint and lingered for a moment on the Colt, which still smoked in his hand. The bigger man's lips curled in an ugly snarl and his gun arm relaxed enough to let his barrel drift toward the ground. From there, the big man opened his massive fist and let the pistol fall to the dirt.

Clint relaxed a bit as well, but wasn't dumb enough to lower his Colt more than half an inch or so.

Jack was walking closer as well and Clint could hear the footsteps like hands pounding on drums.

"Put your gun down, Jack," Clint ordered. "You, too, Laura."

Although Clint couldn't quite hear the woman's steps just yet, he figured that she would be up and raring to go by this time. Judging by the sounds of two solid thumps against the ground, he was right.

There was still a mess to clean up, but for the time being, the fight was over. Even so, there was a gnawing sensation in the bottom of Clint's gut that was telling him something quite different.

SEVEN

Jack stepped up to Clint's side and glared at the big man standing by the empty kerosene containers. "I know this one. He works for the asshole who thinks he can tell me how to run my business."

"What's the asshole's name?"

"Brad Wescott."

The name didn't sound familiar to Clint. "There's a sheriff here, right?"

"Yes." It was Laura who answered.

"Then tell me where he is and I'll take this man to him. I'm sure he'll be interested to know that a fire was almost started here."

Being in such dry country, fires were never taken lightly. Anyone who would start a building on fire on purpose was considered a danger to the entire town and dealt with accordingly.

"So you're just gonna turn this one over to the law?" Jack asked. "Hell, Ed Meeks is barely even a real lawman. He just settles disputes and such until we get around to electing a real sheriff."

"If that's the law in this town, then it'll just have to do," Clint replied. "I'm not about to execute this man if

28

he's willing to end this quietly." Staring intently into the big man's eyes, Clint added, "I may even have to watch over him to make sure that some folks don't stretch his neck on their own once they hear he was about to light a match to this place."

Like most men of his size, the big fellow with the kerosene had a confident look that stemmed mostly from his bulk. Being at gunpoint had taken a bit of that edge from his cockiness. Thinking about the very real possibility of being lynched dulled the rest of that edge real quickly.

Laura stepped up next to Clint and Jack carrying an armful of weapons. "I took the guns from them other two," she said. "One's dead. The other one's still squirming."

Without taking his eyes from the big man in front of him, Clint said, "Jack, sling that squirmer over your shoulder. Does this town have a jail?"

"Yeah. Of a sort."

"Then take him there. I'll follow with this one. We'll figure out the rest from there."

Driver's Town didn't have an official jailhouse, but used an old shack with a sturdy door for the purpose of locking up troublemakers until Ed Meeks could figure out what to do with them. By the looks of it, the shack might have been the first one built in Driver's Town since it was the only one that showed any real signs of age.

Ed Meeks was a tall man with an average build and a head that was mostly bald except for a ring of hair at its base. He lived in the home next to the sturdy shack and when Clint, Jack and the other two men showed up at his door, Ed had nearly run them over in his haste to get outside.

Still pulling on his left boot as he came stumbling through the door, Ed just managed to stop himself before

smashing head-first into the big man being prodded by
Clint. "Jesus Christ," Ed sputtered as he grabbed hold of
the side of the door. "What do you men want?"

Clint peeked around his bulky prisoner and said,
"You're the town law?"

"That's right and I heard shooting, so if you men'll
just step aside and wait here, I'll help you out after I—"

"No need for that," Clint interrupted. "I've got all your
shooters right here."

That brought Ed up short and he took a closer look at
the group in front of him. "That you back there, Jack?"

"Yes, sir, it is."

"What the hell is going on here?"

Since he was a familiar face to Meeks, Jack was the
one who explained what had happened during the shoot-
out and the attempted burning of his stands. Clint was
ready to step in if the truth got too twisted, but he never
found the need to break in on Jack's story. The facts remained pretty much intact, if a bit skewed in the proper
direction.

"I'll have to take a look for myself," Ed said once Jack
was done with the story. "But for now, I guess I should
see these gentlemen into our jail. Are you a witness to all
this?" he asked Clint.

Clint nodded solemnly. "Yes, sir."

Although he didn't seem too happy about it, Ed nodded
and led the way to the shack next door. The locks holding
the door shut seemed as new as the rest of the town, which
gave Clint a sense of confidence that neither prisoner
would be going anywhere too soon. Just to settle his mind
about the matter, Clint took a walk around the shack and
saw there were only two windows. They weren't much
more than slots cut up close to the ceiling and were barely
wide enough for a grown man's fingers to slip through.

"There were plenty of shots fired," Ed pointed out.
"Was anyone . . . uhh . . . hurt too badly?"

"You should probably come see for yourself," Clint said.

As he led Meeks back to the stands, Clint noticed something that struck him as a bit odd. Actually, it was what he didn't see that seemed strange. He didn't see more than a face or two trying to get a look at the source of all the recent commotion.

It was simple human nature to be curious, especially about a fight involving gunfire. But there didn't seem to be many curious people in Driver's Town.

That told Clint that the people were either too scared to look or that they'd seen more than enough fights for them to be curious about this one. Since the smoke had cleared and there hadn't been so much as a raised voice for a while now, Clint discounted the former explanation.

After seeing the way Jack and Laura handled the appearance of those three gunmen, the explanation that remained seemed all the more likely.

EIGHT

By the time they got back to the spot where the fight had taken place, Laura was nowhere to be found. Since Ed Meeks seemed like his head was about to burst after hearing everything that had happened anyway, Clint figured having one less person to deal with was all for the best. As it was, the temporary lawman took in the story, weighed what evidence he could see and came to a decision on his own.

"I guess . . . uh . . . you two can get some sleep and see me in the morning," Meeks said. He paused, nodded and then added, "Yeah. That sounds like what you should do. Neither of you were planning on leaving town or anything were you?"

"Not me," Jack said. "I've got plenty to do here."

Clint shook his head also. "I didn't have any travel plans just yet."

"Good. I guess that'll do for now then, gentlemen. I'll go see to my new prisoners."

Having been in more than his fair share of gunfights, Clint knew that most lawmen liked to relieve both parties of their weapons until things were sorted out. Now Clint was all for living by the law but Ed Meeks acted like someone trying to walk around in clothes that were so big they were weighing him down.

The role of peacekeeper had obviously been forced onto him for one reason or another and Ed was content to just keep things quiet. With the shooting over and half of the fighters either dead or in his makeshift jail, Ed had his quiet. So he turned to enjoy it from his own home.

Clint knew that things were far from over and was glad that Ed Meeks hadn't asked him for his gun. That just prevented any awkwardness, since Clint would have been forced to refuse the peacekeeper's request. After what he'd seen that night, there was no way in hell Clint was going to go about unarmed.

With the peacekeeper gone, Clint and Jack found themselves alone in the street. It had gotten so late that even the glow from the stars above seemed to fade, leaving the light from nearby windows to play across both men's faces.

"I'm just guessing here," Clint said, breaking the silence that had fallen between them. "But those men showing up like that wasn't too big of a surprise to you, was it?"

Jack's face twisted into a shocked expression and he started to put his hands on his hips indignantly. The charade lasted all of two seconds before he abandoned it completely. "No, actually it wasn't. And I didn't want it to be a surprise to you, either. At least, that wasn't my intention. In fact, those boys were part of the reason why I asked you to come out here."

"Well, they're in jail now, so that's that," Clint said, even though he knew damn well it wasn't.

Jack grimaced in a way that made it seem he knew what he wanted to say but just really didn't want to say it. "Well. Maybe it is and maybe it isn't."

Clint rolled his eyes and started walking to one side of the street. For some reason, he was attracting more attention now than when he'd been firing his gun and dodging bullets not too long ago. Once they were out of the middle of the street, Clint stopped and rubbed his eyes. The spent gunpowder was still on his hands and stung his eyes slightly on contact.

"Your letter said that you were starting up a business and that you could use some help in getting it off the ground. At least, that's the way it was told to me. Does that sound right?"

Jack nodded.

"Should I have just assumed that you also meant there were people out to see you dead?"

Letting out a haggard breath, Jack said, "I'd hoped you would come to help an old friend and once you were here, I meant to tell you everything going on. If you'd rather just wash your hands of me, I understand, but I'm in no mood for lectures right now, Clint."

Clint was just about to say something else, but stopped himself when he realized he truly was about to launch into a verbal dressing-down of the distraught man. Rather than give Jack precisely what he didn't want, Clint held back and leaned against a nearby post.

"Fair enough," Clint said after a few moments.

Jack pressed his palms against his face like he was forcing back a holler that would have echoed throughout the entire town. In a restrained voice he said, "And if you don't want any part of this, that's fair, too."

"I didn't say that. This may not be the brightest business decision you've made, but you got a point when you say that it's your right to make it. Besides, I don't take too kindly to folks showing up and taking shots at me no matter how many times it seems to happen."

Suddenly, Jack took his hands away from his face. When he did, his eyes seemed almost bright enough to light the entire street. "What? So you're saying you'll help me finish my racetrack?"

"Not out of the goodness of my heart. I expect to get a taste of the profits once it's up and running."

"Of course, of course."

"And I do expect you to tell me all about whatever you did to get this Brad Wescott so upset with you."

"There's a lot to that story, but I'll be glad to tell it to you."

For a moment, Clint couldn't believe what was coming out of his own mouth. More than anything, he would have liked to keep his life simple and just head out of Driver's Town at first light. There was plenty more to see in Nevada and other friends he could check in on.

But there was the matter of those gunmen who'd showed up with bullets flying. There was no question in Clint's mind that more like them would be back. If Brad Wescott had any kind of money behind him, all he needed to do was hire some more gun hands to finish the job that had been started that evening.

Odds were good that without Clint around, Jack and Laura would be hurt or dead in a matter of days. And if another fire was set, there was a chance that even more folks could be in serious danger. That was most definitely not something Clint was willing to live with.

"Come on," Jack said, his voice filled with newfound steam. "Let me buy you some coffee and I'll tell you the rest of the story."

"Better yet, why not make it breakfast?"

"Well, I'm not exactly hungry and it's a bit late, but I'm sure we could find somewhere that—"

Clint stopped him by waving his hands in front of Jack's excited face. "No. Nothing right now. I'm going back to my hotel room and get some rest and you're buying me breakfast in the morning."

"Oh. Well, I guess that's acceptable."

"It's just going to have to be acceptable, because that's the way it's going to happen." Clint gave Jack a friendly smile and added, "I don't mean to push you around, but I have a feeling that if I let you have your way I wouldn't get any sleep until there's horses running around that track."

Jack started to protest, but wound up shrugging and nodding his head. "Yeah, you're probably right."

"We both need some sleep. Go get some for yourself and we'll take this up in the morning. I came here to help, and that's what I mean to do."

"Thanks, Clint. That really means a lot to me. I don't think I could even tell you how much."

"I'm not worried about that," Clint said as part of him was already regretting getting wrapped up in this business. "By the time this thing gets resolved, I'll think of a good way for you to make it up to me."

Jack grinned in a way that made him look like a bad poker player who'd been dealt a royal flush. "Oh, you'll be plenty happy you stayed. I'd bet the whole Grand Bates Raceway on that."

NINE

Clint was staying at a hotel called the Driver's Inn. Like much of the rest of the town, the place was still so new that the wood of the floors still smelled like freshly cut timber. That, combined with the carvings of wagons and horses over the doors and on the front desk, made Clint feel as though he were still standing outside even when he was walking up the stairs.

The air smelled like it had blown in from a forest and brought a smile to Clint's face. Then again, that smile could very well have come from the prospect of stretching out on a nice bed and getting some sleep. After the night he'd had, that was sounding better and better the more Clint thought about it.

His room was the first one at the top of the stairs. Clint unlocked his door, tossed his hat and jacket onto the bed and was about to sit down when he heard footsteps coming from the hall behind him. He turned around as soon as the footsteps stopped, half expecting to see another gunman. What he saw was something else entirely.

Laura Damon stood in the hallway and took half a step back when she saw the expression on Clint's face. "I didn't mean to startle you," she said, her eyes widening when she saw Clint's hand drop toward his Colt.

Actually, Clint hadn't even meant to reach for his gun. He smiled and took his hand away from the holster. "Sorry about that. It's been a long night and my nerves are still a little twitchy. Are you staying here as well?"

Stepping into Clint's room, Laura walked past him and ran her hands over the nearest bedpost. "I wouldn't mind, but I guess it's up to you."

Clint closed the door and turned to watch as Laura moved around his room. She moved like a cat slinking from one spot to another, getting a feel for her environment before picking a spot to settle into. When she made it to the large window overlooking the street, she placed her hands on the glass and coyly looked back at him over her shoulder.

"If you'd rather that I left," she said, "just let me know. Like you said, it's been a long night."

"What brings you here?" Clint asked. "And for that matter, how did you know where I was staying?"

"Jack hasn't been able to talk about much else since he heard that you'd be coming. He reserved this room for you and bragged about it like he'd invited the president to dinner. Actually, I didn't believe him at first when he said he knew you. Once he started talking about you actually coming to help him out, I thought he'd just hired some gunman to make him look like a big man."

Clint let out a slow breath. So far, he'd been careful not to spread his name around town. In a place the size of Driver's Town, word traveled faster than a runaway horse. Apparently, he shouldn't have even bothered since Jack had seen to it that his arrival was common knowledge anyhow.

"Well," Clint said. "At least now I can see why whoever has a grudge against Jack sent men here armed and ready for a fight."

Curling her bottom lip in an exaggerated, albeit somewhat sexy, pout, Laura turned and rested her back against the closed window. "Oh, don't be too hard on Jack. Not many things go his way, so you can't blame him for getting worked up when something finally goes right."

"Yeah. Tonight really went just perfectly. You sound like you know Jack pretty well. How long have you been partners?"

"Just a year or so. It started with a saloon he wanted to open in Las Vegas and I bought a share using some money left to me by my departed husband."

"You lost your husband?" Clint said. "I'm sorry to hear that."

"Don't be sorry. The only thing that man was good for was driving cattle and cheating on me with any whore he found along the way. I'm just lucky he was thrown from his horse while there was still some money left to his name. Truth is I was set to leave him a month before I even heard he was dead."

Since Clint really didn't know what to say to that, he settled with, "Well, then I guess you're better off without him."

"You got that right. Actually, Jack's saloon idea went off without a hitch. He doubled my money from there. He may be a blowhard, but he gets a good idea every now and then. That's why I've stuck with him for this long." Inching a little closer to him, she added, "I get some good ideas of my own, you know."

Clint could feel the attraction growing between them. Although Laura was still wearing the same thing as the last time he'd seen her, she'd unbuttoned a few of the top buttons on her shirt and her pants were riding a little lower at the hips. Her darkly tanned skin looked smooth and inviting in the room's dim light. The way she moved her hips when she walked was even more tempting.

Although Clint might have been a little worn out after the long day and night, his body was coming awake just

fine the closer she got to him. He met her halfway between the window and the bed, his arms coming out to
settle around her waist. She settled against him as though
that was the very spot her body had been made to occupy.

"What kind of good ideas have you come up with
lately?" Clint asked.

"For starters, I was the one who told Jack to get some
help in taking care of his little problem with Brad Wescott. At least, it seemed little at first." Her hands moved
over his waist and up along Clint's chest. She slipped her
fingers between the buttons of Clint's shirt and worked
them open one at a time. "And coming up here tonight
was another of my ideas."

"I'd have to say that one sounds like my favorite so
far."

"Really? I thought of that one the moment I saw you
stand up to those assholes at the racetrack. They've been
around here a lot and nobody's had the gall to stand toe
to toe with them. Not even that spineless excuse for a
lawman, Ed Meeks."

Lowering his mouth so that he was close enough to
brush his lips against Laura's, Clint spoke in a whisper
that sent a chill through her body, which he could feel
against the palms of his hands. "You're not one of those
people who like to watch blood getting spilled, are you?"

When Laura took in a breath to replace the one that
had been taken away, her breasts pushed against Clint and
she slid her leg against his thigh. "No. I'm a woman who
likes to see a man with backbone. My husband was
the type to run away from a cross word and Jack is . . .
well . . . he's not even the kind of man to put up a fight
when the builders were driven out of town."

Feeling the heat of their bodies growing by the second,
Clint moved his mouth over Laura's cheek and then down
to the side of her neck. His hands were moving as well,

tracing along the rounded curve of her hips and firm buttocks.

"I'd like to hear about what happened with that," he said. "Hearing it from someone besides Jack might be a little more informative."

"And it would take you a hell of a lot less time also. He can barely say his name without taking a few breaths along the way."

Clint smirked at that while continuing to sample her skin with his hands and lips. Her neck tasted sweet and just a little salty. When his tongue flicked against her skin, she tensed slightly and melted farther into his arms.

"So, do you want to talk about what happened to our track?" Laura asked between deep breaths.

Clint's hands slid up and hooked his fingers into the bottom of her shirt. From there, he pulled it open and moved upward to cup her rounded breasts.

"We'll talk about that later," he said. "Right now, I've got some ideas of my own I'd like to discuss."

TEN

Laura let her head fall back and her shoulders relax as she felt Clint take her shirt off. When the material fell away from her body, she leaned back slightly to allow his eyes to drink in the sight of her naked breasts.

Her skin gleamed in the flickering light of the room's lantern, appearing even more smooth and creamy in texture. Clint could feel his own body responding to her. His hands quickened their pace as they moved to peel off more of her clothes.

She let her hands get busy as well, tugging his shirt open and tossing it to one side so she could begin unbuckling his belt. Pausing for a second with the weight of his gun belt in her hands, she smiled excitely when he took the weapon from her and draped it over the back of a chair.

"We won't be needing this just yet," he said.

Laura lowered herself onto the edge of the bed and lifted herself up so Clint could take off her jeans. In moments, they were both naked and she was pulling him down onto the bed beside her.

"What if I get out of line?" she asked mischievously.

"Do you think you might need to draw your gun and get me back under control?"

Clint crawled forward onto the bed while Laura backed away. When her shoulders bumped against the headboard, she reached out to lay her hands across the wooden panel behind her. Clint's hands were moving up over her thighs and he stopped moving forward once his head was near her stomach.

"If you get out of line," he said, reaching out to roll her over, "then I'll just have to use my bare hands on you."

With that, he playfully swatted her backside. The sound of flesh against flesh filled the room, but was quickly lost amid Laura's frantic giggles and squeals. She tried pushing him back with her feet, but he made it through them with ease. Of course, she wasn't trying very hard to keep him away.

Clint and Laura wrestled on the bed for a minute or two; light, friendly smacks here and there interchanging with more lingering touches. Once he worked his way up behind her, Clint reached around to grab hold of Laura with both arms. She was facing away from him and she stopped squirming the moment she felt his body press against her back and his arms wrap around her.

In the quiet that followed their horseplay, the sound of their breathing seemed to fill the room. Laura could feel him shifting slightly behind her and was no longer in the mood to pretend that she was going to resist his advances. Rather than struggle one bit more, she lifted her left leg and moved it back so she could rest it on Clint's hip.

They were both lying on their sides, spooning with naked flesh against naked flesh. Now that Laura had opened her legs for him, Clint could feel his erection grow even harder as the shaft of his penis brushed against the warm moistness of her vagina.

Laura closed her eyes and leaned her head back against Clint's shoulder. "Mmmm. I can feel you've still got some ideas about what you'd like to do."

"Yeah," Clint replied. His arm draped over her side so his hand could drift over her stomach and then down to the patch of hair between her legs. Letting his fingers linger in the dampness there, he added, "It feels like I'm not the only one with that same idea."

Laura was about to say something to that, but lost the words the moment Clint's touch found her clitoris and rubbed little circles around the sensitive nub of flesh. Her pussy got wetter with every circle until her entire body was grinding against his.

"Oh, God," she whispered. "I don't think I can wait any longer."

All it took was a few shifts of his hips for Clint to move the tip of his cock between the wet lips of her vagina. He could feel Laura's entire body tense as he teased her without pushing inside of her. One hand was still rubbing along the upper edge of her pussy while the other was massaging her breast and teasing the hardened nipple.

As much as Clint was enjoying prolonging the anticipation of the moment, he wasn't sure how much longer he could hold out either. But feeling the way Laura moved against him, begging him to enter her with every pleading thrust of her hips, made him want to savor the delicious agony that much more.

Laura reached back with one hand and slid her fingers through his hair, gritting her teeth and making a moaning sound that was filled with pure lust. She hooked the leg that was up and resting on Clint's side even more, pulling him closer while spreading herself open just a little bit more.

That was more than he could bear. The position and motion of their bodies made it that much easier for him to give in to what they both wanted so very much. Clint could already feel the tip of his cock brushing between the lips of her pussy and one more forward push of his hips was all that was needed to slip inside of her.

Feeling him slide into her, Laura arched her back and let out a loud, satisfied moan. Her grip on Clint's hair tightened as she felt him begin to slowly pump in and out of her.

He was now reaching around to wrap one arm across her breasts and he used the other to guide the motion of her hips as he entered her from behind. Laura's muscles tensed each time he entered her and she let out a gasp whenever he strained to drive every inch of himself between her legs. Each time he pulled out, Clint could feel Laura getting wetter between her thighs, making it easier for him to push in again. After a few more thrusts, he began pumping steadily between her legs, their bodies falling easily into a rhythm of straining, sweating muscles and limbs.

The instant Clint took a moment to catch his breath, he felt Laura move away from him just far enough to turn around and push him onto his back. From there, she climbed on top of him and straddled his hips so she could look down at him with a wide, wanton smile.

"Now for that idea that I was getting," she said while moving her hands over his chest.

Clint smiled, enjoying the way her hands felt against his skin. "Oh, I didn't get it quite right, huh?"

"You had it perfect, but this," she said, reaching down to fit him inside of her. "This is what I had in mind the minute I laid eyes on you."

Laura's flesh was warm and fit around him tightly. Straightening her back until she was sitting upright on top of him, she began rocking back and forth, closing her eyes and letting a dreamy smile cross her lips. Her breasts bounced slightly as she rode him, her dark, rigid nipples standing out perfectly.

It felt so good that Clint hadn't even realized that his eyes were closed. He'd simply drifted off into something close to a dream himself and when he opened his eyes again, he watched as Laura began to gently move her hands over her own breasts.

Seeing her pleasure herself while she was riding him made Clint's blood run even faster inside of him. He reached out to grab hold of her hips and just kept his hands there, feeling the way she moved on top of him. The muscles in her body brought intensifying waves of pleasure to him with every movement they made.

Judging by the look on her face and the noises she was making, Laura felt that pleasure just as much as he did. Soon, her hands moved down over her body and onto Clint's. When she felt him pump up into her one time, she dropped forward and supported herself with one hand on either side of Clint's head.

Clint felt her body start to tremble with an oncoming orgasm and when he started to take the lead once again, she was more than happy to follow. Wrapping one arm over her back and pressing his other hand against her buttocks, Clint guided her body while pumping into her faster and faster.

Now that they were both feeling their climaxes start to take hold of them, they wanted only to feel that rush of pleasure overtake them. Laura's breath quickened and she pressed her face against Clint's neck. Every time he entered her, she let out a groan of pleasure that got louder and louder every time.

Clint could feel her tightening around him and when he pushed into her one last time, he exploded inside her with so much passion that he cried out as well. Laura's hips were bucking against him, driving her to a climax that was every bit as powerful as his own and when it was over, she didn't even have enough strength to roll off from on top of him.

Clint reached up once he had the strength and placed his hands on her sides. When he'd started, he thought he was going to ease her onto the bed beside him. But once his hands were again upon her naked flesh, he could feel the first stirrings within him that he didn't want her to leave. Apparently, she could feel it too.

"Are you starting to get ideas again?" she asked.

Clint left his hands on her hips and felt the instant she began to slowly grind back and forth. "I guess this is just an inspirational night."

ELEVEN

The sun flowed in through the big window in Clint's room, bathing every inch with warm light. Having exhausted each other after a night of several more shared ideas, Clint and Laura were lying on top of the mussed covers without a stitch to cover them.

He felt the warmth the moment the sun touched his skin, but was too tired to do anything about it. Laura felt it as well and was in a similar predicament, so she merely nuzzled in closer to him and went back to sleep.

A few hours later, Clint's eyes came open and he reached out for the pocket watch he'd left lying on the bedside table.

"What time is it?" Laura asked lazily.

After fumbling with the watch, Clint studied the simple face. "Nine-thirty. I thought it was going to be a lot later than that."

Laura let out a groan and rolled onto her back. "Too early. Come over here and get back to sleep with me."

But Clint was already out of bed and on his feet, searching for his clothes. "Too early? I'd say it was almost too late. What kind of hours do you normally keep?"

Laura rolled back onto her side and faced him, prop-

48

ping her elbow against the bed and placing her chin in the palm of her hand. Her figure was showcased brilliantly in the sunlight. Every smooth curve was illuminated and she didn't do a thing to cover even one of them.

"I normally get up with everyone else at first light," she said with just a touch of aggravation. "That's why I wanted to take advantage of one of the few times I could sleep in."

"Well feel free to sleep, then. I've got an appointment to keep."

"If you mean an appointment with Jack, then you might want to reconsider. He likes to get his sleep, too, so you might as well get out of those clothes and come back here."

Clint smiled, letting his eyes linger on the slope of her breasts and then on the curve of her hips. "Nice try. I know Jack well enough to suspect that he might not have slept a wink last night after what almost happened to his investment. I'm surprised you're not just as worked up about it."

"Who says I'm not?" Laura asked. "But even I know nothing's going to happen until those gunmen are missed."

Clint gave her a smile that lingered only because it was too difficult to take his eyes off her at that particular moment. "You're a smart woman."

"And I know what I want. You sure you don't want to take a few more minutes with me before you go?"

More than anything, Clint wanted to accept that offer. The only thing holding him back was that he knew he might just want to stay in that room for the next week or so no matter what was burning down outside. "If I don't meet Jack soon, he's likely to kick down this door himself and we wouldn't want that." He stepped closer, ran his hand over her side from hip to shoulder and kissed her behind her ear. "Would we?"

Now Laura was the one who was feeling overly tempted by the moment. She squirmed and clutched the sheets, but kept herself from asking him again to stay, knowing that sometimes waiting only increases the pleasure later.

"Go on then and get," she told him. "I'll find you before too long. Something tells me I won't have to guess to know where you'll be."

His hand was on her backside as he straightened up again, so Clint gave her a playful swat that sounded throughout the room. "Don't stay in here too long. I know Jack will be asking about you as well."

"I know, I know."

With that, Clint turned and left. He shut the door behind himself, lingering in the hallway for a moment or two so he could get a feel for the hotel. In the hours from dawn to noon, there was a certain energy level in a hotel that could tell Clint whether the place was full or empty. He couldn't get an exact feel for it this far after breakfast, but he heard enough people moving around behind various doors to know that the hotel had its share of guests.

That was important because it also told him how many people were visiting from out of town. In a place the size of Driver's Town, there normally wouldn't be too many strangers kicking about. That might change once the racetrack was completed and it certainly would change if and when the railroad ever decided to build a station there.

For the moment, however, Clint got the sense that he wasn't the only stranger visiting at that particular time. Another sound that got him thinking was the rustling and footsteps in rooms three or four, which stopped as soon as the inhabitant got close enough to the door to take a peek outside.

Clint heard the squeak of hinges and turned to look in the hall behind him, but he wasn't quite fast enough. He heard the squeak and clunk of a door closing before he could get a look at which one had been opened. Suddenly, he didn't like the idea of leaving Laura in the room all by herself.

Placing his hand upon the grip of his holstered Colt, Clint went back to his room and opened the door. "Laura, I think you should . . ." But he stopped when he saw that Laura was already up and all but fully dressed.

"You surprised me," she said with a start. "I was just about to head out for some breakfast."

"Then I'll escort you. Looks like we're still having some of the same ideas."

Clint waited while she pulled on her boots and buckled her belt. Laura then took the arm he offered and they both stepped out of the room. This time, Clint was sure to lock the door behind him.

Not only was there still nobody else in the hall, but the entire hotel seemed to be unnaturally quiet as they headed for the stairs and walked down to the lobby. By comparison, the world outside seemed to be a flurry of sounds and motion.

Maybe Jack's prediction that Driver's Town was set to boom wasn't too far off after all.

TWELVE

Clint only needed one guess to figure out where he would find Jack that morning. Without wasting time even glancing anywhere else, he and Laura walked straight to the racetrack site and found him there just as Clint knew he would.

Laura was protesting a bit before they got too close, still demanding something to eat before starting in on the day's business. But Clint would hear none of it and dragged her along until they'd caught Jack's eye. Once that happened, Laura knew it was too late to get away and walked along easily as though she was exactly where she wanted to be.

Jack was standing next to the unfinished stands amid at least a dozen buckets of water. The full buckets were stacked to his left while the empties were discarded in a messy pile to his right. As Clint and Laura approached, Jack was standing with a full bucket in hand. He paused in mid-swing.

"There you are!" he shouted the moment Clint and Laura were close enough to hear. "If you kept me waiting any longer, I was going to use one of these buckets to wake you up."

"No need for that," Clint replied. "I'm here and I brought your partner with me."

"Yeah, I was looking for her, too." With a sly wink, Jack added, "But I knew I wouldn't have to look far once I found you."

Laura rolled her eyes and let go of Clint's arm so she could walk forward and inspect the stands. "Very funny, Jack. Is there a law against me wanting to get some rest and something to eat before I start dealing with this mess?"

"No. But it would have been smart if you would have helped me clean some of this kerosene off before it managed to get lit." As he said that, Jack tossed the water from the bucket in his hand onto a patch of wood that had been soaked with kerosene the night before. "I've been at this all night all by myself and I can still smell the stuff."

Suddenly, Clint felt guilty for being in his room when Jack was out there all night long working. Even as those thoughts ran through his head, Clint got a look at the ground near Jack's feet and the base of the wall. There was some darkening from moisture, but not nearly enough to make him think that a man had been there all night and day dousing it with water.

"So you've been here all night as well as today?" Clint asked.

Tossing away the empty bucket, Jack paused before answering. When he turned back toward the stack to his left, he found Clint already there handing him another full bucket. Lowering his gaze and shrugging slightly, Jack said, "Well, maybe I wasn't here all night. It did take me an hour or two to collect all these buckets this morning, though. Nobody around here will help. Not after all the trouble Brad Wescott's been spreading around."

"I believe that," Laura said as she took up a bucket as well and started walking over to a spot that Jack hadn't yet reached. "Once our builders were run off, nobody else has been too anxious to take their place." She splashed the water and chucked the empty bucket onto the pile nearby. "Some of those poor carpenters were roughed up pretty bad."

Clint walked over to a wall in the stands and ran his fingers over the wood. Kerosene had a slippery texture that was unmistakable even after soaking in overnight and even after being covered with water. For the most part, the wall felt just like wet timber. There were a few places, however, that still felt like the moldy belly of a rock that had been sitting in a lake.

"Just a few spots to worry about," Clint said, pointing out the areas still soaked with kerosene. "I'll help you clean them up and then we can all get something to eat."

"Sounds good to me," Jack said. "I haven't had a bite of food since before you came to town." Although Clint didn't look at him with the same warning glare as before, Jack still winced like a kid who'd been caught in a fib. "All right. Maybe I did have a little something to eat when I woke up, but I am hungry after dragging these buckets all the way over here."

Between the three of them, they got the stands free of kerosene in no time at all. As they worked, Clint couldn't help but notice that the people who passed by tried not to even look in their direction. Whenever they noticed Clint looking at them, the locals would only quicken their steps to take them to where they were going that much faster.

All of the buckets were in the empty pile as well as a few others that Laura had gone to fetch from the closest pump. Clint examined the stands one more time and nodded approvingly. "All done here," he said. "Now let's get something to eat while the both of you tell me why this Brad Wescott decided to become such a thorn in your sides."

THIRTEEN

Jack took them to a nearby steak house that was in between the lunch and dinner crowds. Clint didn't realize just how hungry he was until he got inside and could smell the scent of meat cooking over a flame as well as the aroma of fresh-brewed coffee. They were served quickly by a young woman who wasn't interested in conversation.

In fact, they were served so quickly that it seemed they were being sped toward the door. Before they had a chance to get too deeply into their conversation, rolls and baked potatoes were set down in front of each of them.

"It's like I was telling you last night," Jack said. "No good deed goes unpunished."

Clint swallowed the mouthful of potato he'd been chewing and said, "Yeah. What did you mean by that anyhow? We got sidetracked before you could explain it to me."

Jack shook his head much as he'd done the night before. "I've been repeating that phrase to myself since this all started turning bad."

"Which was about when I came into this whole thing," Laura pointed out.

Ignoring his partner's comment, Jack continued. "Brad Wescott and I worked together on a few deals over the years. He'd always been a good partner and had plenty to contribute. He also seemed to appreciate the plans I came up with for investment opportunities."

Clint smiled at that. "Which means he had deep pockets and was willing to go along with the lines you fed him."

Although his first instinct was to straighten up as if to defend himself, Jack shrugged. He knew that Clint was too familiar with him to be swayed by more fancy talk. "I guess you could say that. But in my defense, enough of my plans worked out that he saw fit to keep our arrangement going for some time."

"So what happened to change things?" Clint asked. "It must have been something, because good business partners don't send gunmen after you to burn buildings down around you."

"I might have thought about it once or twice," Laura said jokingly.

Before Jack could respond, the server came by with the steaks they'd ordered. The cuts of meat were thick and juicy. A little undercooked for Clint's taste, but close enough to what he'd ordered for him to dig in immediately.

As he cut off a piece of his own steak, Jack said, "There's really not much to tell. Brad and I were in business for a while and he decided to strike out on his own. Of course, he was never the visionary that I am, so he couldn't come up with his own ideas. At least, no ideas that would make any money for him.

"I came up with this notion for a racetrack the minute I rode into this here town. You've seen the place, Clint. It's booming all around you and a racetrack will only make it boom more. I'll bet the railroads will want to build a station here before you know it. Not that it matters. Now Wescott is the one acting on my idea all by himself and he's out to make sure nobody else gives him any competition."

Jack leaned forward, took a few quick sideways glances and added, "I've even talked to a man from the railroad myself. He says he'll keep an eye on Driver's Town himself."

"He also said there was a place in Texas that built a town around its racetrack," Laura added. "And the owner of that place now owns a ranch the size of New York. There's no need to be secretive about any of this Jack. Not after you've already bragged about it to anyone who would listen around here."

"Yeah," Jack agreed. "I do tend to get a little over-zealous. But that's only when I've got something good going for me and know it. Also, that was back when folks around here weren't so nervous to talk to me."

"That's something I've been meaning to ask you," Clint said. "From what I've seen, people in this town aren't half as excited about this track of yours as you are."

"It's not their fault. They were plenty worked up when I proposed the idea. They even started an investment society to gather people who wanted to take part in making this town grow."

"So what happened to all of that?"

"Guess."

"Brad Wescott?" Clint asked without hesitation.

"You got it. He and some of his hired hands came here after I started getting more investors and threatened to burn down the home of anyone who lent me a penny for my racetrack. We started building anyway after he left to work on his own track."

"Yeah," Laura said. "That's when things started getting ugly."

"Let's hear it," Clint said.

Jack motioned for Laura to pick up where he'd left off. At least that gave him a chance to eat some more of his steak.

"Wescott didn't even have the guts to show his face here the next time he started trouble," she told him. "He just sent his boys down here to get the builders to leave. They stood their ground, but the men Wescott sent meant business. There was a fight. Some of those carpenters damn near drove those assholes out, but then Wescott's men started shooting." Laura paused as a grim shadow fell over her face. "There wasn't any more fighting after that. Just a lot of blood.

"Not only were the builders forced to leave, but Wescott's men took all their tools and lumber. After that, there was some trouble with the investors."

"What did he do to them?" Clint asked with an angry scowl.

"We don't know," Jack replied. "I know there weren't any fires or anything like that, but that was when folks around here started acting like me and Laura had the pox."

"All right then," Clint said, sawing off another hunk of steak and chewing on it with vigor. "The first thing you two need to do is go talk to your investors."

"But Clint, they—"

Clint cut off Jack with a sharply raised hand. "Just talk to them. You, too, Laura. It sounds to me like they're willing to listen to you, but are just afraid to. After what happened last night, they might not be so scared anymore."

"And what am I supposed to tell them?"

"Tell them it's time to start building up this racetrack instead of letting a half-built stand take up space in their town. Tell them that you want to put their money to work instead of letting it just disappear thanks to some man who thinks he can do business with a gun. Tell them whatever you think you need to tell them, Jack. Just tell them something to get them back on board where they belong. Talking is your strong point, so now's your time to shine."

Clint then turned to Laura. "I want you to start gathering up another team of builders. Charm them, sweet-talk them, bribe them, whatever it takes. Just get them ready to get back to work."

She froze, holding her fork halfway between her plate and mouth. "Back to work? With what?"

"With the lumber that I'm going to bring back here."

"But Wescott took it all away to build his own track," Jack pointed out. "Or maybe he set it all on fire, too. Who knows?"

"I'll know when I go see for myself. And if he used any of that wood for himself, I'll tear it down and drag it back. If he burnt it, I'll see that he pays to replace it."

Both Jack and Laura were visibly stunned.

"What brought this on?" Jack asked. "I know you said you'd help, but . . . all of this?"

"There's another old saying," Clint told him. "In for a penny, in for a pound. I'm in this now, so I might as well be in all the way. Besides, I never was too happy to sit by and watch good people get trampled."

FOURTEEN

Clint talked to Jack and Laura throughout the rest of their meal. He'd heard more than enough to let him know what had happened in Driver's Town and what was at stake. More than that, he'd heard enough to get it straight in his own mind what needed to be done.

Not only did it truly rub him the wrong way that a man with money in his pockets felt free to hurt people and threaten to burn their houses down, but Clint was certain that Wescott was prepared to go even further. By sending out gunmen the previous night, it was obvious that Wescott was ready to see men killed in the name of his own business venture.

Now the racetrack idea might be worthless or it might be good enough to catapult Jack and Laura into the ranks of the rich and famous. Either way, Clint didn't much care. What he did care about was that building the track meant a lot of jobs for a lot of good people. Whatever happened after that was just capitalism at work.

He truly was in this for a pound. He'd seen to that the instant he'd drawn his weapon against the men the night before. If just one of those gunmen got word to Wescott,

Clint's name would be right up there along with Jack's on the other man's hit list.

"Well, let them come," Clint thought as he left the steak house behind and started walking to Ed Meeks's place. "Let them come and see what happens when they try to fight someone who can actually fight back."

Clint wasn't the only one heading out at that moment. After having told Clint where to find Wescott as well as the track he was building, Jack himself was leaving with steam in his stride to talk to the first of his investors.

Jack had been anxious to get to work, but more than a little hesitant as to how successful he could be in the task he'd been given. "I don't know how much you expect from these people," Jack had told Clint only moments ago. "They're scared."

"Well, we'll just have to see what we can do about that," Clint had told him just before leaving the steak house. "Get as many of them together as you can and meet me in twenty minutes."

"Meet you where?"

Clint had told him where to meet and that was that. Laura didn't need any more instruction. Not only was she anxious to do her part, but she'd been chomping at the bit to get started. Now that Clint had lit a fire under them, she was off and running the moment she was through eating.

Now, all three of them left the steak house and scattered like birds that had been flushed from the bushes. Each of them knew where they were going and were anxious to get there. Now that he had the backing of a capable friend, Jack felt like he was closer than ever to accomplishing his goal even though he'd been put behind by a jealous competitor.

Laura got a kick out of seeing a man come in and take action when all she'd been seeing up to this point was a lot of posturing and big talk. Before she was even halfway to the shop of the master carpenter who'd led the crew building the stands, she'd already planned out everything she wanted to say. She had no doubt that she, too, would be able to get some or all of the builders outside to meet Clint in twenty minutes.

As for Clint, he was through talking. Sometimes, the toughest part of a task was committing to it and now that he'd done that, the rest seemed like a trail already laid out in front of him. The only thing that remained was to do what needed to be done, deal with the consequences and not look back.

It was a trail that he was plenty used to riding.

Knowing that the other two were well on their way, Clint didn't look back at them either and kept walking straight to the battered shack that he'd visited the night before. This time, he turned to the little house directly beside the shack, which was where Ed Meeks had been before he came out to receive the prisoners.

In the light of day, the little house looked even more quaint than before. It was a well-constructed home that looked like it belonged more in the middle of a field next to a little rose garden than next to a makeshift jailhouse. Every plank was neatly painted in white while every bit of trim was painted light green. There was even a little picket fence around the house which Clint hadn't seen the previous night.

In contrast, the nearby shack seemed even more squalid and ready to fall down without the night's shadows blanketing it. In fact, Clint was surprised that it could even hold itself up, not to mention hold unwilling inhabitants in.

"Good afternoon," came a voice from the pretty little house.

Clint looked in the direction of the voice and saw the

front door open. Ed Meeks was walking outside holding a cup filled with liquid hot enough to steam in the air, which was still just a bit on the cool side.

"I trust you slept well."

Clint ignored the other man's niceties and raised his voice so he wouldn't have to walk up the primrose path. "I slept fine. How are the prisoners?"

"Would you like to come inside and talk? I made some coffee."

There was something about walking into that quaint little house that rubbed Clint the wrong way at that point in time. Perhaps it was because the house was supposed to be the sheriff's office. Of course, he could have been just as bothered that Ed Meeks was supposed to be the sheriff.

"If it's all the same to you," Clint said, "I'd rather take a look at them myself. Did the one I knocked on the head wake up all right?"

"Actually, I haven't checked on them yet."

"So for all you know, they could have escaped already?"

Ed paused and craned his neck to look at the shack. "Well, it doesn't look like anyone's gotten out of there."

"Mind if I check for myself?"

"Uhh, I should probably do that."

"Then come here and do it. Did a doctor look at either of them?"

Letting out an exasperated sigh, Ed tossed out his coffee and set the cup down gently upon his doorstep. He then made a show of walking outside, closing the door and making his way to the shack. By the way he walked the short distance, someone might have thought he was being forced to march the Trail of Tears.

"Here," Ed said as he unlocked the door. "As you can see, there's nothing at all to worry ab——"

His assurance was cut short by two things: the rush of an oncoming shoulder from inside the shack and Clint's hand roughly pulling Ed out of the way a split second before the sheriff would have been tackled by the escaping prisoner.

FIFTEEN

Clint had to smirk, even as he grabbed Ed Meeks to pull him out of harm's way. He'd heard the rustling inside the shack's door as well as the halted whispering going on inside the makeshift jail. If Meeks had been paying even a little bit of attention, he would have heard it, too.

As it was, Clint considered this a lesson for the peace-keeper. Judging by the wide eyes and open-mouthed gape on Meeks's face, the lesson was well learned.

"Oh my God!" Meeks squealed as the bigger of the two gunmen came out like a charging bull.

Using his left hand to move Meeks, Clint drew his Colt with his right and leveled it at the man rushing out of the shack. Clint recognized the hopeful escapee as the big man who'd doused the stands with kerosene. Clint waited until the man took a few more steps before making his own move.

Once the bull was past him, all it took was a short chop to the back of the neck using the Colt's handle to bring him down to one knee. Clint let Meeks go so he could turn his attention to where it was needed.

"All right," Clint said to the kneeling man. "I think

65

you've had enough exercise this morning. How about getting that other knee down as well?"

When the bigger man didn't comply right away, Clint snapped the Colt's hammer back. Although the movement was unnecessary in order to fire the gun, the metallic click that sounded made its point very well.

The bigger man let out a grumbling breath and bent his other leg so he was now kneeling on both knees.

"You there," Clint said, without taking his eyes off the man in front of him, "in the shack. Come on out. Now."

Ed Meeks was watching all of this from the side and he started shaking his head. "I don't think he can . . . that is . . . he might not be up to . . ."

"He's up and about," Clint said. Raising his voice, he added, "And if he's not, I might as well go in there and finish him off so he doesn't try something like this one here."

Clint was going to wait for the count of five. In fact, he only needed to count to two before hearing shuffling footsteps coming from within the shack. Out of the corner of his eye, he recognized the figure of the gunman who'd done most of the talking from the night before. Clint couldn't see details, but he could tell the other man's hands were raised.

"Come on out of there," Clint ordered. "Ed, you might want to cover him."

"Oh, uh, yes, I would." Ed fumbled for the gun at his side, which he'd damn near forgotten was even there. The pistol looked awkward in his hand, but nonetheless it took away what little steam remained in the prisoner's stride.

Clint took a quick look around. This time he wasn't interested in the town's sorry excuse for a peacekeeper or even the prisoners in Meeks's custody. What Clint wanted to see was the rest of the town. Namely, the people who had been going about their business in a steady flow near and around Meeks's pretty little house.

There were plenty of shops and businesses nearby since everything apart from the stables and blacksmith's shop was on the main street of Driver's Town. At the moment, every eye in the vicinity was trained intently on Clint, Ed and the two prisoners.

All foot traffic had stopped.

There were even a few horses and wagons that had been reined to a stop so the riders and passengers could watch what was going on at the jailhouse shack.

Good, Clint thought. *I couldn't have planned this better myself.*

The truth of the matter was that Clint was certain he could get some bit of commotion started at the shack. What surprised him was how quickly it had all happened. He thought he would have needed at least fifteen minutes to talk Meeks into opening that door.

Clint spent the next couple of minutes making small talk with the prisoners. Of course, to them it didn't seem like idle chatter. They, and even Meeks himself, thought they were talking about what had brought them to Driver's Town and who had sent them. Clint even let the prisoners get some of their pride back by letting them think they might be pulling some fast talk over on him.

In reality, Clint just wanted to wait until it was time for his scheduled meeting with Jack, Laura and whoever else they'd convinced into coming along. Twenty-two minutes later, Clint could see a good-sized crowd gathering nearby. Jack and Laura were among that crowd, which was actually a little bigger than Clint had expected.

"Ed," Clint said in a quiet voice, "get over here." When he saw the easiness in the peacekeeper's walk, Clint added, "And either hold that gun like you mean to use it or put it away."

Having gotten Clint's point, Ed Meeks squared his shoulders, lifted his gun and put on a stern expression. Well, it was as stern as he could manage.

Turning to the prisoners, Clint put his back to the crowd and wore an expression that was all business. His eyes were narrowed and his mouth was set in a grim line. "You two. On your feet."

Throughout their idle conversation, Clint had kept both prisoners on their knees. Now, they both stood up and glared back at the armed men as though they meant to do something about their situation.

"Just what the hell do you think you're gawking at?" Clint asked, his voice nothing like the one he'd used to talk to them before. "You think you can just try to burn this place down and sit on your asses to pay these people back?"

The spokesman started to say something but was cut off by Clint's voice which sparked through the air like a gunshot.

"Where's the court of law in this place?" Clint barked.

For a moment, even Ed wasn't ready to answer. "There isn't one. A judge rides through here every month to hear any cases."

"And what about hangings? Do you get those too often?"

"Hangings?" the spokesman asked. "Now hold on here—"

"No, you hold on," Clint snarled. "Ed here is sick to death of your backtalk and bullshit! Isn't that right?"

Ed was speechless. The expression on his face was almost enough to make Clint laugh, but that was the exact opposite of what he wanted to do at that moment. Clint gave the peacekeeper a subtle nod and prayed that Ed got the hint.

"Yes," he said, catching on just before it was too late to salvage the moment. "I mean *yeah!* I've about had enough of you two."

Although they looked as though they didn't know what

to make of Ed, both of the prisoners were starting to fidget every time Clint looked in their direction.

"If I hear one more word I don't like from either of you," Clint growled loudly enough to be heard by the prisoners as well as everyone watching. "Ol' Ed here might not be able to keep me from hanging you the way I wanted from the start."

The eyes of the spokesman, his bulky partner, as well as those of Ed Meeks widened into saucers upon hearing that.

Clint stepped forward and lifted his Colt until the tip of the barrel was pressed against the bigger prisoner's forehead. "Why don't I just finish you off right here and now? Right in front of these people so everyone can know what happens to troublemakers in Driver's Town?"

"Now just hold on here," Ed said, stepping forward like something close to a real lawman. "I'm the one in charge and I'll say who gets strung up here."

Inside, Clint was smiling. The crowd was eating it up.

SIXTEEN

The moment he saw he had the crowd's rapt attention, Ed Meeks took on the role of hard-assed law enforcer like he was born for it. Close up, from where Clint was standing, it didn't seem quite as convincing, but that wasn't the point of the exercise.

The point was to have the crowd and, to some degree, the prisoners buy into the drama. After walking the streets of Driver's Town and looking into the eyes around him, Clint could tell that the locals were missing something that was very much needed: hope.

Without the people behind them, lawmen or even businessmen didn't have much else to go off of. Clint had seen enough places fall into disrepair for just such reasons and he didn't want that to happen to Driver's Town. If it did happen, they might as well tear down the rest of Jack's racetrack and hand over the mayorship to the next loudmouth with a gun that rode through.

If Clint knew anything from personal experience, it was that there would most definitely be another loudmouth with a gun riding through.

But the more Ed Meeks strutted and barked at those prisoners, the more the locals seemed to draw from it.

Most importantly, the people standing in clusters around Jack and Laura seemed especially interested. Those folks watched what was happening and began talking excitedly amongst themselves. Jack and Laura talked to them as well, hopefully feeding whatever optimism was growing.

Before too long, Clint felt another danger quickly approaching and that was in giving too much of a good thing. "So what should we do, Ed?" he asked when Meeks stopped to take a breath. "Just let them rot in that jail of yours until the judge shows up?"

"I reckon that's what we should do. And if they get out of line . . ."

When Meeks paused to glare at the prisoners, Clint put on a hateful glare and snapped forward just enough for the prisoners to see. That made both of the prisoners jump back a bit. For anyone else watching, however, it seemed that the other men were reacting to the strutting Meeks.

"Get your asses back in there," Clint said to the prisoners. "Or we might just change our minds about letting you see another day."

That was all either of the captives needed to hear. Meeks and Clint had no problem shoving the men back into the jailhouse shack. The confusion on the prisoners' faces, mixed with no small amount of fear for their lives, was priceless. Even Meeks had to work hard to keep the smile from showing up on his face, and when he slammed the door shut, he was greeted by a wave of cheers from the crowd.

Once the commotion was over, people began to get back to their activities, with everyone, including the groups that Jack and Laura had brought, heading in different directions.

Meeks started walking back to his little house, but he stopped before passing through the gate of the picket fence. "I don't know exactly what that was all about," he told Clint, "but I appreciate it."

"That was about winning a few cheap points of respect among the people you're supposed to be watching over."

"Thanks for that, Mr. Adams."

"Don't be too grateful. This is just to get you started. To keep that respect, you'll have to work for it. Keep an eye on those prisoners and for God's sake, hire some deputies."

"I'll do that. What about you?" Meeks asked, his face brightening. "Would you like the job? I'll bet you could teach me plenty."

Clint was tempted by the offer, but only out of a sense of responsibility to finish what he'd started. "I'll keep that in mind, Ed. For the moment, though, I've already got plenty on my plate without adding any more."

"Well, the offer still stands if you change your mind. This town is booming." Ed paused, took a breath and let it out as though he was only starting to believe the statement he'd just made. "Even if I'm not the man to act as law around here, Driver's Town will need someone to fit the bill sooner or later."

"I think you'll do just fine for now, Ed. And with a bit of practice, you might just convince yourself that you're the man for the job after all. I'd say we convinced everyone else."

"Yeah. We just might have."

When Clint left, he knew he'd made a difference. There was a part of him that thought Ed Meeks might just have the stuff to be a lawman when it was all said and done. After all, everyone had to start somewhere. At the very least, Clint figured the place would stay together until he got back.

SEVENTEEN

As Clint walked to the stables, he deflected any questions about the scene at the jailhouse by directing whoever was asking them to Meeks. That way, he did his part to make Meeks seem even more like the man in charge. If the fuse on that powder keg was going to remain unlit, that was the way it needed to be.

After arriving at the stable where Eclipse was waiting, Clint took his time saddling the Darley Arabian and getting the stallion ready to ride. By the time he was about to leave, Clint saw Jack come running up to his stall with a wide smile on his face.

"I know you told me a bit about what you wanted to do," Jack said, "but that was even better than I could have imagined."

"It looks like you did a good job yourself. You got quite a few people to follow you down there for that show. How'd you manage it?"

"There was a board meeting for the town's business committee about to take place and I walked in like I owned the place. I convinced them that the Grand Bates Raceway wasn't such a lost cause and that they needed to take another tour of the property. Not many of them

73

were convinced that it was such a good idea, so I came up with something on the spot."

"I hope it wasn't too big of a lie."

Jack shrugged. "Then maybe I should tell you about it. Anyway, the important thing is that they do have an opportunity to profit still, right?"

"Yes, I imagine so. What did they say about what happened at the jail?"

"They couldn't believe their eyes! They were even talking about officially electing Ed Meeks as sheriff."

"I didn't hear talk as grand as that," Laura said as she strode into the stables and came up close enough to pat Eclipse on the snout. "But the builders I brought sure weren't so afraid of what Brad Wescott had sent here."

"That was the whole point of it all," Clint said. "You did a good job of getting the right people there to see it yourself. How'd you manage to drag so many out for me?"

Laura shrugged and winked at Clint. "Easy. I told them I wanted to buy them all a drink and took them the long way to the saloon."

Jack shook his head and suppressed a laugh. "Why the hell didn't I think of that?" he grumbled.

Without missing a beat, Laura answered, "Because you're too used to fast-talking and your straight-talking has gotten a little rusty."

"I think she's got you there," Clint said.

Laura turned to Eclipse and patted the Darley Arabian on the neck. The stallion responded to her instantly, nuzzling her hand and making a contented sound in the back of his throat.

"This is a fine animal," she said. "He looks fast, too."

Clint slung his saddlebags over Eclipse's back and climbed onto the stallion's back. "He's fast enough to get me to where I need to go in a hurry."

"Remember," Jack said. "Wescott's place in a huge

spread half a day's ride outside of Las Vegas. Just head toward Vegas and you won't have any trouble finding it. The name of the town should give it away."

"He's got a town to himself as well?" Clint asked. "Maybe I should consider moving down here and starting a town myself. What's his called?"

"Wescott. The town's called Wescott." Jack shook his head and added, "I have a hard time believing a man could be so full of himself."

Laura rolled her eyes and gave Clint a wink while nodding toward Jack. "I don't."

Jack didn't try to figure out the sly insult that had been aimed at him. Instead, he was already trying to figure out what would happen two steps ahead of where he was. "So what should we be doing while you're gone? And when will you be back?"

"You two just keep doing what you're doing," Clint said. "Get those investors back on your side and get those builders ready to go to work. We may have gotten their confidence up today, but there's plenty more that needs to be done.

"As for your other question, I'll be back when I'm finished. However long it takes to get those supplies and that lumber back here, that's how long I plan on staying away. I also need to have a talk with this Mr. Wescott about his poor manners."

Clint took up his reins and got Eclipse moving toward the stable's front door. Looking over his shoulder at Laura and Jack, he told them, "Just be sure to be ready for me when I come back."

With that, he was off and running.

EIGHTEEN

Driver's Town was about a day's ride or so northeast of Las Vegas. Since Clint hadn't known there was a town called Wescott in the area, he was just going to have to take Jack's word for it. Besides, with the personal experience he'd had in dealing with big-headed businessmen, Clint didn't have any trouble believing that one thought himself worthy of having a town named after him.

In fact, he was sure there were plenty more where Wescott came from.

After being in the stable for a few days, Eclipse was more than ready for a run. The stallion moved like a wave of muscles beneath Clint's saddle, each motion flowing into the next like thunder rolling through the sky. Actually, Clint was just as ready as Eclipse for the ride and found himself smiling widely the moment the horse hit its stride.

Once he'd pointed Eclipse's nose southwest, all Clint had to do was snap the reins and hold on. For the duration of the ride, Clint would have been hard-pressed to think about business ventures and double-crossing partners or even the machinations of greedy men.

Despite the fact that he'd been put face-to-face with all

of those things and more, Clint was too wrapped up in
the simple joy of riding to bother himself with things he
couldn't change at the moment. That was the secret to
dealing with big problems and not breaking under the
pressure. A man had to know when to worry and when
to just partake of the pleasures life was giving out at the
moment.

Just then, riding was the pleasure of the moment and
Clint was partaking to the hilt.

There would be plenty more time for the underside of
life once he got where he was going. The big problems
weren't going anywhere without him.

Clint stopped that night to make camp and sleep beneath
the stars. With autumn quickly approaching, the night sky
seemed especially clear and those Nevada stars spread out
over him in a way that they just didn't seem to do anywhere else. Once he had settled in for the night, Clint just
leaned back, taking in the stars until sleep claimed him.

All in all, it was a relaxing night and he was up early
the next morning. By early evening on the second day
after leaving Driver's Town, Clint was riding into Wescott. Eclipse hadn't eased off until they were only a few
miles away, as if the stallion had sensed when a comfortable stable stall was nearby.

Clint was happy to oblige and put the horse up in the
nicest of the two stables he spotted on his way into town.
As a reward to the Darley Arabian, he had even sprung
for the better greens and tipped the stable boy in advance
to make sure Eclipse was well cared for. In the back of
his mind, Clint also knew that he might very well need
to pull out of town in a hurry if things didn't go well with
Brad Wescott, so Eclipse needed his rest for that as well.

The sun was approaching the western horizon when
Clint walked out of the stable with has saddlebags slung
over one shoulder. He took his time following the direc-

tions the stable boy had given him to one of the better
hotels, gazing at the town itself as he moseyed along.

Right away, Clint could tell that his presence in town
had not gone unnoticed. Everywhere he looked, he could
see locals staring back at him. They were either wary of
strangers or just wary of him in particular. Tipping his
hat to the people he saw, Clint got plenty of nods in return. They were quick nods, to be sure, but friendly all
the same.

That led him to believe that the locals simply didn't
see too many unfamiliar faces strolling through their
town. There was a cautious look in the people's eyes that
shone through even when they smiled nervously at him
from the other side of the street.

More than once, Clint noticed a hand drifting toward
a holster when he was spotted, but nobody went so far as
to threaten him openly. Perhaps these people were a little
warier than he'd first thought. From what he'd seen of the
town during his stroll, Clint had a good guess as to why
that was.

NINETEEN

After coming from Driver's Town, Clint had been expecting Wescott to be at least somewhat similar. Most of that came from all of Jack's talk that Brad Wescott was trying to do such a similar thing in putting a racetrack in a town that was set to boom. But Wescott had plenty of differences when compared to Driver's Town.

Mainly, Wescott was bigger. That struck Clint as soon as he'd started walking through the place. But more than that, it seemed like a newer town had been built around an older one. As he took in the sights, Clint saw older streets and buildings situated in and around the newer ones. In theory, this shouldn't have been much different than any other town that had grown since its founding. But the differences between the old and new in Wescott were so drastic that they were striking.

The new buildings were ornate and well maintained while the older ones had been allowed to decline without the slightest bit of upkeep. As such, the businesses in the older buildings seemed on the verge of going under. Windows were broken, doors swung lazily on their hinges and workers sat around without much of anything to do.

The locals that were shopping or visiting restaurants

were only doing so at the newer places. Clint noticed several uncomfortable glances being thrown toward the older storefronts, but those people kept right on walking to the newer places and tried not to look back.

By the time Clint made it to the Desert Spring and checked into his room, he got the distinct impression that not only was it policy for the newer businesses to be patronized, but it was enforced. He'd spotted a few men making rounds in a way that a lawman might do at the end of his day. But the men wore no badges and they glared at the locals with either antagonism or straight-out aggression.

His room was nice and clean since the Desert Spring was a newer hotel. The prices were high for a hotel without so much as a bar or restaurant inside, but Clint dropped his bags there anyhow. Now that he'd arrived and gotten a lay of the land, he had better things to do than haggle over the price of his room.

On his way down to the lobby, Clint stopped at the desk where he'd checked in and approached the middle-aged man behind the register.

"Any thoughts on a good place to get something to eat?" Clint asked.

For a moment, the clerk's face brightened and he seemed about to launch into a well-worn reply. But before he got a word out, he stopped himself and cleared his throat. "The Winner's Circle," the man told him. "Place just opened up."

Nodding, Clint said, "Seems like half the town just opened up."

"Yeah, well with the racetrack on its way, we're bound to grow even more before it's all said and done."

Clint nodded, studying the other man without being too obvious about it. To him, the clerk appeared to be talking as if reading from a script. His hands clutched the edge of the desk and his feet shifted as though he wanted to be anywhere else besides where he was standing.

The clerk might have noticed that Clint was watching him for the last second or two, or he might have just realized that he wasn't doing a good job of appearing to be relaxed. Either way, he forced himself to let go of his desk and put on a somewhat more convincing smile. "Try the Winner's Circle, Mr. Adams. You must have had a hard ride and they even serve food along with beer and liquor. There's ladies there to relax you as well."

"All right, you convinced me. The Winner's Circle it is. By the way, is there a telegraph office in town?"

"Yes, sir. Two streets north of here and one over."

"Thanks for your help. I guess I'll be going now."

Clint said that last part just to see what the other man's reaction would be. As he'd guessed, the clerk seemed visibly relieved to hear that Clint was leaving. So much so that some of the color even flowed back into the other man's cheeks.

"The Winner's Circle is just around the corner. You can't miss it."

"Thanks again." Clint could only imagine the clerk's relief would grow the moment he stepped out of the hotel.

Imagining the clerk's relieved sigh as he walked outside, Clint turned in the direction he'd been pointed and started walking. Although he hadn't been planning on doing much drinking or gambling while in town, Clint knew he was being herded toward the Winner's Circle. As welcoming as that might have sounded on the surface, he doubted he was being led there for any comforting reason.

There was something else weighing on Clint's mind at that moment, however. Mainly, it was why the hotel clerk seemed to know who he was. Clint had been careful not to introduce himself to anyone in town and when he'd signed the register, he'd only left his initials.

Those things, coupled with the odd feeling he'd gotten since his arrival, didn't sit too well in Clint's stomach. As far as he could tell, the prisoners sitting in Ed Meeks's jail had never been given the opportunity to send any messages to tell their boss what had happened or what they'd found in Driver's Town. Clint knew that if either of the prisoners had been allowed out to send a telegraph, they would have more than likely escaped altogether.

Perhaps he was being overly optimistic, but Clint also figured that Meeks would be too busy playing the tough lawman role to cut the prisoners any slack. Clint had also recognized the fear on Meeks's face when that bull of a man had tried to charge through him.

No, Meeks wasn't going to let either of those men out anytime soon. He would use Wescott's telegraph to verify that himself, but Clint decided there must have been other eyes and ears looking in on Jack and his associates. With that thought in mind, Clint recalled the footsteps he'd heard in the hallway outside his hotel room at the Driver's Inn.

That rock was still churning in Clint's gut and he didn't think it would stop anytime soon.

TWENTY

Despite all the things he'd heard about this Brad Wescott, Clint certainly had to hand it to the guy about one thing. He sure knew how to run a saloon.

From what Clint could see, the Winner's Circle was the bright spot of the entire town. The sun had dropped beneath the horizon when he walked over to the saloon, and in the growing darkness, the Winner's Circle seemed to radiate warmth and energy. The music coming from the place was wild and merry and the voices coming from there were pretty much the same.

By the time he was close enough to smell the cigar smoke drifting out from over the batwing doors, Clint couldn't help but be anxious to get inside and see what all the fuss was about firsthand. He didn't even have time to study the outside of the saloon for more than a second or two before he was swept inside along with a throng of people headed in the same direction.

The saloon itself wasn't the biggest Clint had ever seen, but there was enough going on inside the place to fill several buildings. It even had two bars and two stages. Each bar and stage set were smaller than average, but they were positioned on opposite ends of the room, to completely surround the guests.

As the name implied, the place was laid out in such a way as to make Clint feel like he was in the midst of a celebration the moment he walked in through the door. The bar closest to him was on his left, while a narrow rectangular stage was nearby on the right. On the other side of that stage was the second bar and next to that bar was the second stage. Scattered throughout the middle of the circle were tables set up for dining and gambling in equal measure.

If the town had seemed a bit empty and standoffish when he'd first arrived, that was more than made up for by the hospitality of the Winner's Circle. Clint hadn't been there for more than a minute or so, but he had already been offered a drink and gotten a good look at a line of dancing girls kicking on stage.

In all, it was a bit overwhelming at first, but Clint quickly adjusted. The first step to calm his nerves was to accept a drink from the closest bartender who'd shouted at him the moment he came through the door. By the time Clint actually found a place to stand at the bar, his beer had been poured and was waiting for him like an old friend.

It wasn't the best beer he'd tasted, but it was cold and did wonders to wash away the dust that had collected at the back of his throat after his ride. Better yet, when he tried to pay for it, the bartender merely shook his head and waved the money away.

"First drink's on the house for first time visitors to the Winner's Circle," the bartender said.

Clint lifted his glass and replied, "Much obliged."

"Compliments of Mr. Wescott."

"Any idea where I can find him so I might thank him personally?"

The bartender didn't answer right away. It wasn't that

he didn't hear, which would have been perfectly understandable considering the ruckus inside the saloon.
Mainly, he seemed surprised that anyone would ask that
question at all.

"Mr. Wescott is over at his normal table," the bartender
finally said. "Just look for the biggest group of dancing
girls that aren't on stage."

Clint craned his neck around to see if he could spot
what the bartender had been referring to. Although he was
doubtful at being able to find Wescott right away, seeing
that the whole place seemed packed with dancing girls,
Clint actually didn't have any trouble whatsoever.

There was easily a girl or two for every man in there,
but the women clustered around a card table close to the
second bar were all dressed in the flashy, sequined uni-
forms of the girls on stage. Not only that, but they were
easily twice as beautiful as the rest of the girls milling
throughout the room.

Clint took a sip of his beer and started fighting his way
through the crowd. He'd managed to arrive in town and
at the saloon right when the night's crowd was starting to
grow. As such, he was jostled several times by drunks,
gamblers, working girls, locals and waitresses alike.

The closer he got to Wescott's table, the more attractive the women seemed to get. Their dresses were made
of a filmy material that clung to the curves of their bodies
like water flowing over their naked skin. Even though the
skirts came down past their knees, there was still plenty
to see. In the right light, the material was close to trans-
parent, leaving little to Clint's imagination. For some of
the girls, the only thing keeping them from being exposed
through the gauzy fabric was a few well-placed sequins.

Smiling to himself, Clint maneuvered to Wescott's table and muttered to himself, "It's good to be king."

TWENTY-ONE

The moment Clint broke through the ring of onlookers, hangers-on and women surrounding around Wescott's table, he was spotted by the main man himself. Wescott wasn't hard to spot. Besides being the center of attention, he was the one dressed like a man who was rich enough to name a town after himself.

Brad Wescott appeared to be in his early fifties and had a head full of thinning black hair. He wasn't a large man by any stretch of the imagination, but he carried himself as though he were bigger than the entire saloon. His eyes were wide open and dark, but seemed to Clint as though they were narrowed into slits. Perhaps that was because of the intense furrows on his brow or the power behind his stare.

"Ahh, Mr. Adams," Wescott said. "How nice of you to join us. Please, take a load off."

Since he didn't have a shot of blending into the crowd anymore, Clint stepped right through the rest of the people crowding him and walked up to the large round card table. "I'd be happy to have a seat, Mr. Wescott, but there aren't any open ones nearby."

With a scowl directed to a chubby man at Clint's right,

Wescott created a place for Clint to sit. The moment he saw that scowl coming his way, the chubby man couldn't get up from his seat fast enough. He didn't go far, however, and stayed less than an arm's length away from where he'd been sitting.

"There you go," Wescott announced happily. "Ask and ye shall receive. That's what I and the Good Book always say."

Nodding slightly, Clint took the chubby man's seat. He did not miss the fact that Wescott blatantly put himself before the Good Book. Even though Clint wasn't exactly a religious man, he knew there was plenty going on behind that little statement.

Wescott waited for Clint to be seated before saying, "You must be tired. After all, it is a healthy ride from Driver's Town."

The fact that Wescott recognized Clint on sight, knew he was coming from Driver's Town and seemed to have been expecting him were all surely designed to provoke a reaction. Clint recognized that fact by the smug look on Wescott's face as he'd showed his cards one by one. But Clint refused to play into whatever game was being played and simply acknowledged the statements as they arrived.

"It was a bit more of a ride than I was expecting," Clint said. "But I made it easily enough. By the way, thanks for the beer."

"Not at all, Clint, not at all. It's me that should be thanking you. I appreciate the fact that you came all the way out here to talk to me man-to-man instead of taking the word of some piker who got his nose put out of joint."

Wescott watched to see what reaction that might get. Again, all he got was a noncommittal shrug from Clint.

Inside, no matter how much he tried to push it back, Clint was most definitely feeling an effect from Wescott's words. Just because he knew what the other man was trying to do, that didn't mean that he could suppress every reaction he had. Clint still felt a sting from Wescott's smug smile and barbed comments. The fact that he knew so damn much already didn't sit too well either.

"If you don't mind," Clint said, keeping a neutral tone, "I'd like to speak to you somewhere a little quieter."

With Wescott still glaring and his eyes fixed on his target like a hunter behind his rifle, the rest of the crowd around the table seemed to fade away. Indeed, the saloon itself seemed to quiet down. "But I just got here, Mr. Adams. I'm not a man who likes to be pushed around in his own saloon, not even by someone with a reputation like yours."

"I'm not trying to push anyone anywhere. All I want is to talk business someplace where I can hear myself think. I just thought you were a businessman who might appreciate the same."

"I am a businessman, Mr. Adams. More of a businessman than your friend, Jack Bates."

Clint didn't move much. Just a shift in his chair that caused him to lean more forward upon his elbows. But that, combined with the sudden fire that flared up in his eyes, was more than enough to make Wescott and everyone else around that table take notice.

A good deal of them, Wescott excluded, even backed up a step.

"I know this is your place," Clint said in a voice that was just a shade away from being a snarl. "I know most of the buildings around here are yours. It's not too hard to get that since this whole town is named after you. I don't care if you quote the Good Book or if you wrote it, I won't have you talk to me like I'm just another dog that shakes when you raise your voice."

"Mr. Adams, I'm not accustomed to someone threatening me in—"

"Yeah, yeah," Clint interrupted. "You said my name

enough so everyone knows who I am. Well, I'm getting a good picture of who you are as well. By the way, if I was to threaten you, you'd know it and I guarantee that you wouldn't be laughing it off."

Those words hung in the air for a few moments. Now, more than ever, the noise level inside the saloon seemed to fade away to nothing. The girls still danced on both stages and the people at the bar still downed their drinks and told their jokes, but around Wescott's table it had gotten as quiet as a funeral service.

Wescott's face was hard as stone and just as unreadable. None of the people around him wanted to do or say anything until they got a cue from their boss as to which way to jump. Finally, that cue came in the form of a serpentlike smile that crept over Wescott's face.

That smile quickly widened until it seemed almost jovial. "You're a brave man, Clint Adams. Apparently, that part of the stories about you was true. I'll talk business with you, but not until I do what I came here to do."

"What's that?" Clint asked.

"This is a poker table. I came to play poker."

Clint nodded, tipped back his beer glass until he'd drained all of it and set the glass down onto the table. "I think I'll pass, Mr. Wescott, but thanks all the same."

For the first time since the conversation had started, Brad Wescott seemed taken aback by what he'd heard. He started to say something in return, but couldn't get out more than a grunt before Clint had gotten up and turned his back on him.

"I'll find you when you're done playing," Clint said. He could almost feel the steam coming from under Wescott's collar as he left.

TWENTY-TWO

It took every bit of Clint's strength not to laugh as he walked away. Even though that surely would have gotten one hell of a response in itself, Clint figured he'd stirred up enough just by cutting off Wescott's display before what was probably meant to be the icing on the cake. Turning his back on the almighty important businessman was just a fun bit of insult added to injury.

Clint walked away from the card table and headed for the front door. Rather than leave the Winner's Circle just yet, however, he decided to stick around for a bit and watch some of the aftershock of his arrival and subsequent departure.

He didn't have to wait long before he was approached by the same bartender who'd been so friendly when Clint had first arrived.

"I don't know what you said over there, mister," the bartender said in a hurried whisper, "but it sure didn't look good from where I was standing."

"Well what the hell do you know? All you could see is the top of Brad's hat."

That statement didn't come from Clint. In fact, Clint was almost as surprised to hear it as the bartender who

90

was looking around to find the source of the comment.

He didn't have to look far. The one who had spoken up came striding forward and stopped at a spot at the bar directly next to where Clint was standing. It was one of the beautiful dancers that had been standing around Wescott's table. But, in Clint's opinion, she was by far the most alluring woman in the room.

She stood a few inches shorter than Clint, yet carried herself so she could look him directly in the eye. Her posture accentuated the impressive curves of her hourglass-shaped body. Wearing one of the filmy sequined dresses favored by the dancers, she filled out hers better than any of the rest. In fact, her solid, voluptuous build put every other female in sight to shame.

Smiling at Clint in a sly, sexy way, she shook back some of the blond hair that had fallen in front of her face and extended her hand. "Hello there. My name's Rachel Cleary."

"I'm—"

"I know. Clint Adams," she cut in with a laugh. "Brad said it only about three dozen times. I think you're the most well-known man to walk in here and he wants to make sure everyone knows it."

"Does Mr. Wescott need another round of drinks?" the bartender asked.

"No, and he's not even looking over here, so you can stop trying to look like a good dog."

It was natural enough for the bartender to be angered by that, but he kept himself in check and found something to do somewhere else. Clint turned and leaned one side against the bar so he could get a better look at the blonde.

With a body like hers, the sequins on her dress weren't able to do a very good job of covering her. Instead, they added a sparkle to the veiled curve of her breasts. Wide, generous hips that were wrapped in a silk black skirt shifted beneath the gauzy material.

"Did Wescott send you over here?" Clint asked.

"No, but I'd be looking for one of his boys to be coming for you any moment."

"Then what brings you over here?"

She smiled and looked away as though she knew she shouldn't say what she was about to say. When she lowered her head slightly, that stray lock of golden hair fell down across her face again. When she looked up and tossed the hair aside with a flick of her head, her breasts shook enticingly beneath the sequins.

"I wanted to come over and see if you were the genuine article or just some fellow with a death wish," she said.

"You've had your look at me. What do you think?"

"I think you've got steel nerves, that's for sure. I've never seen anyone waltz in here as you did and talk to Brad Wescott like that. Do you know that you might just be living on borrowed time for doing what you did back there?"

Clint smirked. "I hear that a lot and I always seem to borrow more time."

"I'll bet you do." Rachel was looking him over just as much as he'd been studying her. Judging by the sparkle in her eyes, she liked what she saw. "Can I ask you a question?"

"I'm not about to stop you."

"If you did ride all this way to get here, why would you act like that? Plenty of folks that want to talk to Brad don't even get a chance to sit down with him."

"Because Brad wasn't about to talk to me. He just wanted to swat at me until I took the bait."

She smiled even wider and started nodding. "You're a smart man, Clint Adams."

"That depends on who you ask. You might change your mind about that before too long."

"Maybe." Rachel's eyes darted away from Clint for

just a moment before coming back to rest upon him like fiery sapphires. "I just hope I get the chance to spend more time with you so I can find out for sure."

Clint didn't have to ask what she meant by that. He was good enough at reading people to easily pick out the doubt in her voice that she would be seeing much more of him at all. Not only that, but there was a bit of a warning in her voice as well, mixed with just the slightest touch of fear.

But Clint didn't even need to read all of that to know that trouble was coming.

He could see that much in her eyes.

Those eyes that were like clear, polished sapphires.

TWENTY-THREE

In his years of dealing with women, Clint had learned that the best lesson of all was to look into their eyes whenever possible. Gazing into a woman's eyes could give a man insight as to what she was thinking, what she wanted, or even what she desired. It could even tell him when he was in trouble.

Of course, that last part was mainly true because of Rachel's special kind of eyes that not only glittered with promise, but reflected some of the shapes moving around her.

Clint spotted the motion reflected in her eyes and could make out just enough to know that a figure was rushing up on her. That meant that same figure was rushing up on Clint from behind and that, combined with what she'd just said to him, got Clint moving like a trap that had just been sprung.

He grabbed the first thing he could wrap his hand around, which was the glass being held by a drinker standing nearby at the bar. It was taller than a shot glass, but not quite as big as a liquor bottle and fit nicely into Clint's grasp as he closed his fingers around it.

Twisting at the waist, Clint pushed Rachel down with

his free hand and pulled himself around in a tight, quick semicircle. The figure that had been rushing toward him was a man grasping a stiletto in one meaty fist. As Clint spun around to face him, the attacker's eyes went wide in shock but it was too late to do anything more than plow forward.

Even if the attacker had wanted to stop, he didn't have enough time to do so before Clint's hand came into contact with the side of his head. That was exactly the way Clint had planned it.

Twisting his body until it was sideways to the attacker, Clint felt the skinny blade scrape past him and the glass in his hand shatter against his palm. The glass was solid enough, but Clint had put enough force behind his swing to break it against the other man's temple.

With blood gushing from the fresh wound in his scalp, the attacker dropped like a stone and let the knife slip from his hand.

Clint was still in motion, even though his assailant was no longer a threat. The hand that had been pressed against the top of Rachel's head snapped to one side and plucked the stiletto from the air before it could damage anything or anyone on its way to the floor.

Straightening up, Clint offered a hand to Rachel and helped her up. He flipped the stiletto in his hand while saying, "And here I thought the policy in this place was to be polite to newcomers."

Rachel reached up to straighten the hair that Clint had mussed and looked at him with a smile as wide as a canyon. When she looked down at the man lying bleeding on the floor, that smile only got wider. "That was amazing," she said. "I've never seen anyone move that fast."

"Well, I've got you to thank."

She was beaming as she looked at Clint and then back down to the man who'd attacked him. Twisting around and struggling to see through the people that had gathered around at the first sign of the quick scuffle, Rachel could only get fleeting glimpses of the table where Wescott had been sitting.

Clint was crouching down to get a look at the man he'd dropped. Sure enough, it was the chubby fellow whose seat he'd been given. The fat man groped at the floorboards and kept trying to get up, but was still too dizzy to do anything more than flop right back onto his behind.

After one more failed attempt to get his feet beneath him, the fat man reached for the gun at his side instead. His hand didn't even make it halfway before something came crashing down onto his wrist and pinned his arm against the floor.

That something was Clint's boot.

"Here's some advice for you," Clint said, glaring down at the fat man. "Stop trying to please your boss and start trying to get on my good side. I'm the one that's closest to killing you right now."

Just as he'd wanted, Clint saw the fat man's eyes turn wide with fright.

"I was just supposed to hurt you," the fat man said quickly. "Honest. I swear I was just supposed to cut you a bit to put you in your place."

Clint took his boot away and took the gun from the fat man's fingers. From there, he stood up and started walking toward the door. He was stopped by a strong grip around his elbow.

"Not that way," Rachel said while tugging on his arm. "Come with me."

TWENTY-FOUR

For the moment, Clint figured that walking one way out of a beehive was just as good as another. If a trap was to be sprung, surely someone like Wescott would know to have more than just the front door rigged. Besides, he was curious to see what Rachel had in mind.

She led him the long way through the saloon. Although they were spending more time inside the place than if they'd just stepped out through the front, the crowd was stirred up enough to keep them covered most of the way. Every time they were jostled by another body, Rachel pressed hers against Clint and smiled at him one more time.

By the time they were at the back of the saloon in a space between a bar and a stage, Clint was very familiar with the blonde's body as well as her smile. Truth be told, he wasn't the least bit tired of either.

"I heard Wescott telling his boys to wait for you outside," she said to Clint. "They'll be wanting to hurt you even more for showing him up twice in his own place."

"Where are you taking me?" Clint asked.

"This door leads to some back rooms used by us dancers. We can change or just put our feet up between numbers."

"Does Wescott know about it?"

"The only thing he cares about when it comes to his dancers is that they keep dancing and they keep hanging on him like he's God's gift."

Clint was wary about where he was being taken, but allowed himself to go there all the same. Once he realized that the man who'd sent those gunmen to Driver's Town already knew he was there, Clint figured everything after that was a danger to his well-being. He could think of worse ways to go than on the arm of someone as stunning as Rachel Cleary.

Besides, so far it looked like she was telling him the truth.

Just as she opened the door, a stampede of light footsteps came racing toward them from the direction of the stage. Clint turned to look and was immediately swarmed by a mass of smooth, fragrant flesh wrapped up in thin silk and sequins. He and Rachel allowed themselves to be carried through the door by the wave of dancers and soon felt as though they were miles away from the saloon's main room.

Compared to what he'd seen of the Winner's Circle, the backstage area felt like a dark, shadowy haven. The voices and commotion of the main room could still be heard, but they were muffled through layers of wood and curtains.

"Come on," Rachel said, taking Clint by the hand and leading him down with the remaining flow of dancers.

By the looks of it, both stages were changing dancers at the same time. Either that, or it just felt that way since the hallway they were in was fairly cramped and tight. Clint kept his wits about him and was ready for just about anything.

Suddenly, he was pulled slightly off balance as Rachel

tugged him through one of the narrow doors they'd been passing. The door swung almost all the way shut and the rest of the dancers kept walking by, chattering amongst themselves and primping for their next set.

Rachel kept herself pressed against him, looking up into his eyes with an excited expression until the noise backstage had died away to a low rumble of motion behind the walls and doors. Her hands were on his arms, running up and down until she was rubbing his shoulders.

"I've heard of you, Clint Adams," she whispered. "If you're really the man I've heard about, then you might be able to do this whole town a big favor."

With Rachel so close to him in the small, dark room, Clint was unable to keep himself from letting his own hands wander as well. The filmy dress that Rachel wore was just a bit of silky texture that didn't stand in the way of him being able to feel the smooth glide of her skin or the firm muscles of her hips and back.

"You shouldn't believe everything you hear," Clint told her. "Especially when it comes to barroom gossip concerning street fights and such."

"Oh, this is about more than just street fights. One of the girls was talking about you just before you showed up. She used to do shows in Wyoming and said that she got to spend a few very good nights with you."

"Is that a fact? What's her name?"

"Sara Wilson."

The name sounded vaguely familiar, but it had been a while since he'd gone through Wyoming. Of course, Clint did have a few memorable dancers that sprung into his mind. There was another question that concerned him more than the other girl's name, however. "You said she was talking about me? How'd my name come up?"

"Brad Wescott was boasting to all the ass-kissers he plays cards with that you were on your way and that Jack Bates must be really foolish if he thinks sending one man against all of his men was going to do any good. Even," she added, pulling in a breath and tracing her fingertips over the muscles of Clint's back, "if that man is the Gunsmith himself."

"Do you know how he found out about me?"

She shook her head. "All I know is what I heard around that table. He doesn't pay us girls too much mind, but if he thinks we're listening in on him, he gets awfully cross."

Clint took a look around. His eyes had adjusted to the darkness, but he still couldn't see much of the room they were in. Then again, that might have been simply because there wasn't much to see. "Where are we?"

"Just a little room used for storage. Nobody uses this place much and hardly anyone even really knows it's here. Sometimes, us girls come back here for a bit if Brad or one of those pigs he hires wants more than we're willing to give."

"Is there a way out from back here?"

"Yes, but you might want to wait awhile. After what you did at the bar, they'll be looking for you. They'll probably lose interest in a bit, though. At least they should ease up enough for you to slip out the back way without being seen."

Clint slid his hands down her back and cupped her strong, rounded buttocks. Lifting her up off her feet, he turned and pressed her back against the door, which was the only door he could see in the entire room. "Then how do you suppose we should pass the time?"

TWENTY-FIVE

Even as he supported her weight between himself and the closed door, Clint slid his fingers up underneath the thin black skirt Rachel wore. The skirt was actually more of a slip and between his insistent fingers and her squirming, the material came easily up over her hips.

Rachel was working as well. The moment she felt Clint pick her up and push her against the door, she was busy tugging his belt open and pulling open his pants. From there, she slipped her hand down between his legs until she could wrap her fingers around his erect cock.

The moment she touched his penis, she could feel it getting even harder. Rachel's heart started beating faster in anticipation and her breathing became quick and heavy in his ear. She could feel him pulling her skirt higher up around her waist and then pull her panties aside with such force that he nearly tore them off her completely.

As soon as Clint could feel beneath the silky material of her undergarments, he rubbed his fingers gently down between her legs until he reached the warm thatch of hair that was waiting for him. She was already damp and as he teased her clit with a few gentle strokes, Clint's fingers became even wetter with her moisture.

The next thing Clint felt was Rachel's legs tightening around him and her hips shifting so that her pussy was positioned just right to accept him. As soon as she was ready, she guided him into her and arched her back against the door as every inch of his swollen shaft was driven in between her thighs.

Now that he was inside of her, Clint moved both hands onto her buttocks and gripped her tightly as she started to writhe against him and he began pumping in and out. Her face was directly in front of his and she stared right into his eyes as he fucked her. Every so often, Rachel's mouth would open as if to speak, but she only let out a gasping, straining breath.

She had one hand running through his hair and the other was holding on to his back, her nails scraping against his back. Unable to hold back any longer, she moved her head forward so she could kiss him fiercely on the lips. Her mouth opened and her tongue quickly found Clint's, both entwining in a way similar to how their bodies were entwined.

Clint could feel her muscles straining in his hands and against his body. Her legs clamped around him with such strength, that he doubted he needed to hold her up any longer. But her backside felt so good in his hands that there was no way on earth he was going to let her go.

Rather that let out the moans that were aching to come out of her, Rachel kept her mouth pressed against Clint's and allowed herself to make little noises as he kept driving into her. His thrusts felt so good between her legs that she couldn't help but dig her nails even deeper into his back. If she'd had her way and they were both completely naked, she might have even broken the skin.

Clint could feel the pressure of her nails against his shoulder blades and couldn't deny the erotic pleasure it gave him. She responded instantly to every move he made. When he ground his hips against her, she held on tighter. When he leaned back so he could get a look at her finely toned body, she opened her legs for him and pumped her hips back and forth over his cock until she thought she might explode.

For a moment, Clint almost forgot they were trying to keep quiet. When he leaned forward, he tightened his grip on her buttocks and pounded into her one time with enough force to slam her back against the door. Rachel's eyes widened with excitement, begging him to pump into her harder still, but Clint struggled to hold back.

Well, he held back as far as making more noise was concerned.

Slowing his rhythm down to a stop, he started easing her down and away from the door. Rachel took the hint and dropped her feet so she was standing when he let go of her. Their bodies broke contact for just as long as it took for her to spin around, press both hands flat against the door, spread her legs and present her luscious backside to him.

The only reason Clint paused was to take a look at the view in front of him. Rachel stood leaning against the door, her skirt hiked up around her waist and her naked back covered only by a thin layer of sequins and silk. Her blond hair flowed over her neck, stopping just at the top of her shoulders.

Clint moved his hands flat against her sides, kneading her flesh as he moved in closer to her. His penis was rigid, aching to be inside of her and it fit perfectly between her thighs. He slid it against her wet vagina once without entering her while his hands moved up over her ribs.

Rachel looked over her shoulder at him and was about to demand that he stop teasing her when suddenly his hardness was once again filling her up. Every nerve in her body tingled as he slid inside and his hands reached around to cup her breasts.

Pumping forward with his hips, Clint massaged her full

breasts with both hands. He could feel her tensing even more than before, now that his cock was rubbing her from a new angle. When he closed his thumbs and forefingers around her nipples while entering her again, Clint felt Rachel press back against him as she tossed her head back.

The breath that escaped from her lips was loud and lingering, filling the room with the sound of her approaching orgasm. He was pumping steadily now and she was writhing in time to his increased rhythm. When her climax approached, it did so quickly, overtaking her like a landslide of pleasure that coursed through every inch of her.

The longer and more powerfully Clint thrust, the closer he got to his own climax. Entering her from behind, he could feel Rachel's round backside bumping against him. His hands were still cupping her breasts and all he could see was the delicious curve of her spine beneath the sequins.

Suddenly, Rachel dug her fingers against the door with so much power that she almost left marks in the wood. Her orgasm was so powerful that when her muscles clenched around Clint, it drove him over the edge as well.

Clint pushed all the way inside of her, climaxing when he couldn't enter her anymore. He stayed that way for a few moments, lingering inside of her until he gathered the will to leave her warm embrace.

When she felt that he was no longer inside of her, Rachel turned and wrapped her arms around Clint so she could press her lips against him for another passionate kiss. At that moment, Clint wouldn't have minded hiding out in that little room for days.

Maybe even weeks.

TWENTY-SIX

A few minutes later, there was another rumble of light footsteps coming from the hallway outside. Clint and Rachel stayed inside the little storage room until the footsteps passed. Listening to the dancers flow by toward the door leading out to the stages, Clint had his ear pressed against the door and his body against Rachel.

Every move she made got him thinking about anything but the task at hand. Judging by the sensuous, mischievous look in her eyes, that was exactly what she was trying to do.

"That'll be the last of them," she told him after a moment of silence. "The next show's starting. We might want to wait just a little longer in here. You know. Just to be safe."

Although the way she moved her fingers over his chest was definitely having an effect on him, Clint pushed it aside as best he could. Since that wasn't working too well and he didn't have any cold water handy, he did the next best thing and opened the door they were leaning against. First, he opened it just enough to get a look outside. When he saw the coast was clear, Clint stepped into the hall and waited for Rachel to follow.

She did so, albeit somewhat grudgingly.

"Maybe you're not as much fun as I heard," she chided.

Clint gave her a little pat on the backside to quicken her pace and said, "Well, I'll make it up to you later. Now how about showing me the back door out of this place?"

Once again, Rachel took him by the hand and hurried along. She led him farther down the hall in the direction where the dancers had all been running earlier. Now that every space wasn't filled with a running person, the hall seemed a bit more spacious. It was still a far cry from wide open, however, and the longer Clint walked down the dark passage, the more confined he felt.

Finally, they got to the end of the hall where there were three doors waiting for them—one to Clint's right, one to his left and one straight ahead.

"Head out that way," Rachel said, pointing to the door to the left. "It'll drop you at the back of the building. You know where you're going from there?"

"Yeah. I'm staying at the Desert Spring Hotel." Since it was no secret to Wescott where he was staying, Clint figured there was no harm in letting anyone else know.

"Mind if I pay you a visit later on?"

"I'd mind it more if you didn't. I'm in room number two."

"All right, then. I'll see you later. I'd best get back before Brad notices I'm gone. As soon as the show starts, he'll be wondering where his own private dancers are. Then again, he might just be too wrapped up in looking for you to notice."

"Thanks for your help, Rachel," Clint said after opening the door and taking a quick look outside. "I really appreciate it."

She shrugged and started walking back toward the door leading to the main room of the Winner's Circle. "You probably didn't need it, but I didn't want to see a man like you get hurt. After all the grief Brad Wescott has given to this town, I'm sure I won't be the only one that might lend you a hand."

"True, but you might be one of the few that have the guts to try anything against him."

"Take care of yourself, Clint Adams. I'll be real disappointed if you're not around when I come looking for you later."

Clint watched her go and only took a moment to admire the enticing sway of her hips. Even in the shadows of the backstage hallway, the sequins of her dress and the natural light tone of her skin and hair were easy to follow. The hard part was taking his eyes off of her.

As he stepped outside, Clint was thinking about what Rachel had just said. She'd mentioned disappointment, which was something that was on his mind as well. So far, he didn't have a good reason not to trust Rachel apart from the fact that she kept company with Brad Wescott. That might not be her choosing, of course, so he couldn't rightly hold that against her too much.

That just left the general distrust Clint felt when dealing with new people in dangerous situations. When there were high stakes involved, people had a tendency to pick sides real quickly. With the type of money that Brad Wescott had and the investment that Jack and Laura had already put up, the stakes were high, indeed.

Both sides of this had lots to gain and plenty to lose. Apart from all of that, Clint already knew that someone in Driver's Town had been feeding information back into Wescott's ear. With all that in mind, Clint figured he was more than justified in being just a bit cautious when it came to new faces.

But there was something about Rachel that made him want to trust her. More than just her beauty, it was something in Clint's heart that always hoped for the best in people. All too often, people did the wrong things just because they were easier. Seeing someone throw in on the right side for any reason every now and then did him a lot of good.

Disappointment wouldn't have begun to cover it if Clint's suspicious mind turned out to be completely right yet again. There was some comfort to be had from being wrong. Especially when it came to being wrong about the badness in people's souls.

More than any of that, even more than what he'd learned from his own experiences, Clint had learned to listen to his gut. For the time being, his gut was telling him that Rachel wasn't the biggest threat to him at the moment. So far, she'd even seemed genuinely interested in helping him.

Even though he'd just met her, she hadn't steered him wrong yet although she'd had plenty of opportunities to do so. Glancing around the back lot and nearby alleyways as he put the Winner's Circle behind him, Clint could tell that most of the men who appeared to be looking for him were, indeed, concentrated at the front of the saloon.

That was another good mark in Rachel's favor. Clint figured he'd find out where she stood for sure when she came to see him later on. In the meantime, there was plenty of other business to take care of.

TWENTY-SEVEN

The night was still fairly young when Clint found his way out of the biggest saloon in Wescott. There was still plenty of commotion coming from the Winner's Circle and even more activity on the streets nearby. In fact, the longer Clint watched from the shadows, the more the streets seemed to come alive with motion and the sound of figures pacing back and forth.

He was an excellent judge of character and could read plenty about another man just by watching his eyes or the way he moved. Clint watched the men he recognized as the ones that had been clustered around Brad Wescott like the businessman's own private army. They'd seemed plenty tough inside the saloon on their own turf, but some of that was starting to fade now that they were out in the open.

Clint could tell the men patrolling the street weren't looking overly hard to find him. That was why he had been sure to drop the fat man inside hard and fast, so everyone could see. From what he could tell, that fat man was still on a lot of people's minds because the previously cocky hired guns now seemed more anxious to get back to their cards.

Of course, that didn't mean that they were going to abandon their jobs. It just meant that nerves were on edge and each of the gunmen had grabbed an extra pistol, rifle or shotgun to supplement the weapons they already wore.

Clint shook his head as he watched the gunmen walk along the street. He was standing in the shadows around the corner only two buildings away from the Winner's Circle. Although he wasn't in plain sight, he shouldn't have been that hard to find. The tension in the air was so thick that he could taste it.

Those men didn't need more guns. They just needed the wits to be able to use the ones in their holsters.

Even after his little break with Rachel backstage, Clint could see that the gunmen were only just starting to widen their search beyond the Winner's Circle and its immediate neighbors. Most of the men were headed toward the other end of the street, which would take them to the hotel district. A few were staying behind to poke their noses into the darker corners nearby, so Clint held back and waited for one of those to get just a little bit closer.

The man headed his way looked to be slightly taller than Clint with about ten to fifteen pounds of added muscle. He reminded Clint of one of the big men that had tried to burn Jack's stands down. Apparently, Wescott put a lot of stock in raw muscle. Perhaps the businessman wasn't as smart as he thought he was.

Clint shifted back into the shadow just a little bit more, listening intently to the sound of approaching footsteps. The other man moved just like a big man. His feet slapped against the ground like hooves and even his breathing seemed to be a rush of noisy wheezing. Clint figured he might have been able to close his eyes and still get the drop on the bull coming his way.

Of course, the big man didn't share that opinion. In his mind, he was big and that was all that mattered. Otherwise, he would have taken more care when looking for someone who'd already proved himself to be dangerous. But the big man wasn't thinking about any of that as he came stomping toward the corner where Clint was waiting.

The man barely had time to think about much of anything before Clint's hand shot out from around the corner and grabbed hold of him by the front of his shirt. The big man started to raise the shotgun he'd been holding, but that had already been plucked from his hands despite the iron grip he had on the weapon.

Using his left hand to take hold of the bigger man, Clint pulled him off his balance and grabbed the shotgun with his free hand. The man was a little bigger than he'd been anticipating, so Clint abandoned any hope of taking the shotgun away by force. It was still an easy matter of twisting and applying pressure to the right spots.

No matter how strong someone was, their thumbs were always the weakest part of their grip. Clint knew this and twisted the shotgun one way as a feint and then pulled it against the other man's thumbs with a short burst of his full strength. That was enough to take the shotgun away from the big man, and before his opponent could react, Clint had the shotgun's barrel pressed up beneath the bull's chin.

"Don't worry," Clint said. "I don't want to kill you. That is," he added, thumbing back the shotgun's hammer, "unless you don't leave me any other choice. You got me?"

The big man's eyes burned with rage and his body was tensed for action, but he knew better than to do anything just yet. Instead of giving in to the violence that was running through his head, he simply nodded and kept that burning glare fixed on Clint.

Clint saw the acknowledgment, but kept himself ready to react at a moment's notice as well. Rather than put any distance between himself and the big man, Clint stepped in closer so the bull wouldn't have a chance to draw back for a swing or make any other powerful motions. Without the ability to cock back a fist or swing back a leg, the bull effectively didn't have much in the way of horns.

"I want you to go back to that saloon and do just what you were supposed to do," Clint said.

"I'm supposed to find you and hurt you." There was more emphasis put on the last part of that, which caused the bigger man's lip to curl.

"Well then, you'll have to settle for one and not the other. When I let you go, you can run back to Wescott and tell him you found me. I also want you to let him know I just want to talk some things over. Business things. He should like that."

"You could have done that in the Winner's Circle. Why didn't you just play cards with him and talk there instead of busting up Fatty like that?"

"Because I'm no stranger to a card table. Your boss didn't just want to talk. He wanted to get a chance to read me, get a feel for my style and personality so he could gain an advantage. Then he could talk business thinking he's got the upper hand. That doesn't sound fair to me."

The big man seemed confused by what Clint was saying, but he was doing his best to remember the words. Clint could tell that much by the furrowed brow and overwhelmed look in the other man's eyes.

"Does Mr. Wescott do a lot of business while playing cards?" Clint asked.

The bull tried to nod, but was brought up short by the gun barrel under his chin. So instead, he grunted, "Yeah."

"I'll bet a lot of those deals come after a few hours of cards, and they always come up in Mr. Wescott's favor. Am I right?"

"Yeah."

"There you go. You just give Mr. Wescott my message. Have him meet me at my hotel so we can discuss business on an even field. Think you can do that?"

The bull started to grunt again, but stopped himself. Instead, he forced a nod that butted up against the end of the shotgun.

There were more searchers coming toward the spot where Clint and the big man he'd captured were hiding. Like the bull who had come before them, the others stomped noisily ahead, somehow fumbling in the right direction.

Clint could hear them and, judging by the way his eyes were straining and he fought to keep quiet, the big man could hear them, too.

"Go on then," Clint said, starting to move away. "Tell Wescott what I told you and we can both be on our way."

But that wasn't going to happen.

The bull had made his decision and it wasn't in Clint's favor.

TWENTY-EIGHT

With just the notion that there were reinforcements nearby, the big man lost all the complacency that had been in him before. Suddenly, he didn't seem so worried about Clint or either of the guns in his possession. The only thing on the bull's mind was doing the original job he'd been given so he could try to salvage some of the pride he'd lost along the way.

"Hey!" the bull shouted. "I got him, right over—"

He was cut off by a quick, short jab from Clint who tapped the shotgun up against the other man's jaw. The shot wasn't much of a jab, but it was placed just right to knock the other man's teeth together, snap his head back and put a little bit of wobble into his knees.

Clint swore under his breath as he delivered the jab. When he saw the bull's eyes rattle in their sockets for a second, he took a quick glance around the corner to see if anyone was coming and how many there were. Taking his eyes from the other man wasn't what Clint wanted to do, but it was necessary and he wagered that he could do it quick enough to avoid any repercussions.

He was quick, but not quick enough. The repercussions, on the other hand, came quicker than Clint might have expected.

Since he was still close to the big man, Clint was unable to see as the bull snapped his fist up and delivered a jab of his own. The big man was quicker and more coherent than Clint had bargained for, and the short, upward punch toward his groin came as a most unpleasant surprise.

It was all Clint could do to keep from falling over. The pain that lanced up from below his belt was like a fire that scorched all of his nerves at once and blazed up to form a screen of red behind his eyes that temporarily blinded him. Luckily, the punch had landed a few inches higher than the bull had intended.

With his adrenaline fighting to compensate for the pain that burned below his belt and in the depths of his stomach, Clint pulled in a deep breath and shook the red haze from his vision. Just as it was clearing, he could feel something large and solid slapping against his chest and knocking him backward like a leaf in a stiff wind.

That solid thing was the big man's hand, which pressed flatly against Clint's chest. With a flex of his muscles, the bull shoved Clint away from him until Clint's back was roughly introduced to the nearest wall.

For the moment, all thoughts of pain were flushed from Clint's head. That moment came when he saw the bull's fist coming toward his face like a speeding train. Clint was just able to squat down before his face was wrapped around the bigger man's fist. He could feel the shock waves of the impact through the wall and heard a jarring crunch as the bull's knuckles slammed into wooden planks.

Clint knew that unless he wanted to shoot the big man, he would have to act quickly. With the option of gunfire ruled out for the time being, that put the fight squarely on the stronger man's turf. All of this flashed through Clint's mind in less than a second. Even before the thought was completely formed, he'd already started making a move to tip the scales back in his direction.

The shotgun Clint had taken had a barrel that had been sawed off to a more manageable length. That left a few feet of wood and steel for Clint to work with. Hunkering down a little more, he threaded the gun between the big man's legs and turned it sideways like a clasp being closed on a cuff link.

Then Clint straightened his knees and shot straight into an upright stance. The top of his head knocked against the big man's chin and the shotgun swept both of the bull's legs right out from under him.

The big man landed with a thunderous impact that was almost loud enough to drown out the sound of his approaching reinforcements. Most of the air rushed out of his lungs once the bull hit the ground, but he still had plenty of strength in him to look up and start struggling back onto his feet.

He didn't have enough strength to keep awake, however, when Clint sent the stock of the shotgun into his temple.

Clint winced when he slammed the wooden end of the shotgun into the big man's skull simply because he'd done so with more force than he would normally use. Not wanting to take the chance of prolonging the fight, Clint put some extra steam into his blow and hoped some of the impact would make it through the other man's thick skull.

The bull's head snapped back and started to come upright. His eyes blinked several times and, for a moment, it appeared as though he might even start to stand up again. But after a gushing exhale, his eyes glazed over and his head dropped back against the dirt.

Clint could hear the other men approaching and knew they would be rounding the corner at any moment. Rather

than try to avoid the confrontation, Clint took it head-on
and leapt around the corner himself to see what was coming.

Sure enough, there were three men closing in fast with
another two lagging fifteen to twenty feet behind. Clint
swung the shotgun around and paused for a second to
make sure everyone in front of him could see what he
was packing. The moment he saw the look of fearful rec-
ognition in the eyes of the closest men, Clint squeezed
both of the shotgun's triggers.

Fire erupted from both barrels and the shotgun lurched
like a living thing in Clint's hands. The blast roared
through the night and sent a plume of smoke churning
outward toward the oncoming men. The shot itself went
low, however, just as Clint had aimed.

If he was going to deal with Wescott in any way, Clint
wanted to avoid killing his gunmen unless it was abso-
lutely necessary. Scaring them out of their wits, on the
other hand, was a pleasure.

The three men forgot the guns in their own hands once
Clint's shotgun went off, and they tripped all over themselves trying to get out of the line of fire. By the time
they realized that the only thing hit was the ground a few
feet in front of them, Clint was already gone.

TWENTY-NINE

Clint wanted to stop by his room after backtracking through the streets for half an hour or so. After putting the search party behind him, he'd slowed his pace to a slow jog and then a normal walk. Since he'd already drawn more than enough attention to himself, he didn't see the use in drawing any more.

There were some people out and about, but most of the locals were either in their homes or had found a nice place at a bar or gambling table for the night. That made it easier to spot the men that were looking for him, but Clint wouldn't have had any trouble spotting them anyhow.

Like an occupying army, Brad Wescott's men strutted about with their weapons drawn as though they owned the earth beneath their feet. Clint avoided them easily enough and made it back to the Desert Spring without incident.

He was greeted by a friendly nod from the desk clerk, a different man from the one who'd checked him in, and he walked up the stairs to his room. Clint's mind was split about fifty-fifty on whether or not there would be someone there waiting for him. He made sure to be ready for the worst and drew his gun just outside his door.

After unlocking it and opening it a crack, Clint stepped to one side and then pushed the door open the rest of the way. It banged against the wall and started to swing back. Apart from that, there wasn't one more bit of noise.

Still cautious, Clint walked inside and didn't lower his guard until he'd lit both the room's lanterns and checked beneath his bed. Apart from that spot, there wasn't any other place for someone to hide, so Clint let out the breath he'd been holding and dropped his Colt back into its holster.

It didn't take long for him to gather all his things since he really hadn't unpacked any of them to begin with. Mainly, he took the time to rest up after his busy night and got himself ready to move on. He was sitting at the small table in his room checking over his modified Colt when he heard the very sounds he'd been waiting for.

Someone was walking the hall just beyond his door. The steps were soft and somewhat cautious since they stopped and started again several times. Finally, they settled in a spot not too far from Clint's door, but not directly in front of it, either.

The next thing he heard was a knock on the door directly across the hall from his room. Clint snapped the Colt's cylinder shut and slid it into its place at his side, but didn't take his hand from the pistol's grip. Walking on the balls of his feet, Clint barely made a sound as he walked across the room and to the door.

Whoever was outside was knocking again and Clint used that sound to cover the sound of him opening his door a crack and peeking outside. Checking over the register while signing it had long become a habit when Clint checked into a hotel. Because of that, he knew there wasn't anyone staying in room number two.

That was why he'd given that number to Rachel when he told her where he was. The fact that she was now outside knocking on room number two showed that she was either an impeccable listener or that she truly hadn't been sent by Brad Wescott, who would most definitely know that Clint was in room number three.

The fact that Rachel was alone in the hall also spoke a good deal in her favor.

Clint opened the door just a little bit more so he could see the hallway down toward the top of the stairs. There was nobody else waiting there either. Clint opened his door all the way, announcing his presence while finally taking his hand away from his gun.

"Oh," Rachel exclaimed while turning around with a start. She had an embarrassed smile partially on her face, which turned to shock when she saw Clint standing in the other doorway. "Didn't you tell me you were in this room?" she asked, pointing to door number two.

Clint smiled at her and shrugged. "My mistake. Good thing I caught you before you gave up and left. Come on in."

Although she seemed a little suspicious at first, that seemed to disappear before Rachel even stepped through his door. "I guess it's understandable enough," she said. "You have had one hell of a night."

Clint had stepped out to clear the doorway so she could walk by. While he was out there, he took a moment to glance up and down the hall one more time. He still couldn't find a sign of anyone else.

Of course, that didn't mean that they weren't on their way.

"Yeah," he said, stepping back into his room and shutting the door. "And it looks like it won't be slowing down anytime soon."

THIRTY

Rachel was no longer in her dancer's dress. Although Clint missed the sheer fabric and the sequins, the tantalizing curves were still very evident beneath her more conservative attire. A simple, yet elegant red dress fell over her generous breasts and hips in a way that accentuated them even more than when they'd been on display beneath sheer silk. The neckline was high, but a slit in the material formed an oval-shaped opening which started at her throat and moved down low enough to give a nice taste of cleavage.

Upon entering the room, she went to the bed, past it, and straight to the window, which was hidden behind a set of drawn curtains. She was careful not to open the curtains too much as she took a peek outside. "You shouldn't be here," she said.

"I take it you heard about my little scrap outside the Winner's Circle?"

Laughing as she turned around, Rachel said, "The men Brad sent out after you came running back inside like scalded dogs. Anyone close to his table heard what they said. I was going to wait awhile before meeting you, but after I heard, I got over here as soon as I could slip away."

"That might not be the safest thing to do, you know."

"I know. But I couldn't look at myself in the mirror if I just let Brad do what he wants to do and not come here to warn you."

Clint stepped forward and placed his hands on her shoulders. Not only did Rachel seem earnest in what she was saying, but her body was trembling with nervous energy.

"Come on," he said. "This place isn't too safe for either of us."

"Then why are you here?" she asked, her voice suddenly taking on a scolding tone. "I can talk my way back into Brad's good graces, but he'll hurt you, Clint. He might even kill you."

"I just needed to get my things and catch my breath. Besides, Wescott won't move against me again so soon after what happened here and in Driver's Town. He'll have to hear the story from his men, sort through the truth, holler at whoever needs hollering at and then he'll start asking around to find out exactly where I am."

"How do you know all this?"

"Let's just say this isn't the first time I've had someone after me. Wescott's the type who wants others to fight for him. He may carry a gun, but he'd rather stand behind an army than fire a shot on his own. I could see that much in his eyes."

She shook her head and stepped up close enough to wrap her arms around him. Even without being able to see nearly every inch of her through sequins and silk, Clint could still feel the curves of her body and the soft warmth of her pressed against him.

"After all this is done," she said, "do you think you could take me with you?"

"With me where?"

"Anywhere away from here."

"You can do that on your own, Rachel. You don't need

me or anyone else. So far, you've proven that and then some."

"I know, but I'd like you to take me." Her hand wandered over his chest and then drifted briefly between his legs. "I don't think I've had enough of you yet."

"We won't be able to do much of anything if we're dead," Clint told her. "And that's what both of us could be if we stay here any longer."

She gave him a kiss and stepped back. "You're right. It's just that I feel like nothing can hurt me just as long as I stay close to you."

"That's funny. It seems like close to me is usually where all the shooting is. But you're welcome to your opinion. Now come on. We've got to get out of here."

He took her by the hand and practically dragged her out the door. The thought had entered his mind that Rachel was keeping him there on purpose. After all, the message he sent with Wescott's man was to meet him at that hotel. She might have known that and she might not have. For the moment, Clint still wanted to go along with his plan of action. Whichever way Rachel was leaning, he thought it best to keep her close.

With the blonde in tow, Clint headed out his door and straight for the stairs. He didn't hurry, but he wasn't about to dawdle, either. He just kept a brisk pace and his eyes open. Anything could happen at any time. Knowing that, Clint wasn't about to be caught off his guard.

Before leaving, Clint handed the desk clerk a folded piece of paper. On it was a message that he'd prepared not too long before Rachel had arrived. It was a note for Brad Wescott and when he handed it over, he did so after leaving Rachel by the door so she couldn't see exactly what he was doing.

If she was telling him the truth, then the less she knew, the better.

If she was trying to herd him into a trap, then the same also applied.

Clint's suspicions were growing darker the more time he spent in Wescott. Thankfully, he doubted he would be there much longer.

"If Mr. Wescott or any of his men comes around asking for me," Clint told the desk clerk, "just give them this note."

"I will, Mr. Adams."

"And do me a favor," he added, handing over a few folded dollar bills. "Don't tell him when I left or who was with me."

The desk clerk nodded, but didn't take Clint's money. He leaned a bit over the counter and said, "I've heard about some of the hell you've been raising, Mr. Adams. Are you planning on keeping it up?"

Clint had been expecting plenty, but this wasn't on his list. "That was my idea."

"Then keep it up and keep your money. Seeing Brad Wescott or any of those sons of bitches on his payroll get their noses bloodied is payment enough."

"Much obliged, but at least keep the money for the room."

"Room?" the clerk asked, looking around as though Clint's voice had come from nowhere. "I didn't rent a room. I can't recall much of anyone coming through here since I started work."

Clint nodded and gave the clerk a wave as he left. It was nice to get a good surprise every now and then.

THIRTY-ONE

Clint and Rachel walked across town hand in hand like any other couple walking the streets at that time of night. Granted, there weren't many other couples walking the streets at that time of night, but what few people they saw along the way didn't seem to take much notice of them. The few that did merely tipped their hats and kept on moving.

After seeing the way Brad Wescott's men strutted around town, Clint figured he might get support from the locals who just wanted to live in their town and go about their business. That was part of the reason that Clint headed toward one of the older looking sections of town.

He thought people there would be closer to the way things used to be before Wescott had come in and slapped his own town on top of the first. Also, Brad Wescott struck Clint as the type of man that was so self-centered he might not pay too much attention to what went on in the sections of town where his own mark couldn't be seen.

Clint had spotted a hotel on his way into town and kept the place stored in the back of his head. He went there now and found the door locked and no lights behind any of the windows. There was a rope hanging beside the door with a little sign hanging beside it that read, PULL FOR SERVICE.

Tugging on the rope caused a bell somewhere inside the hotel to ring and soon there were heavy footsteps clomping toward the door. Clint could hear the grumbling of whoever was removing the latch and prepared a smile for when the door finally was pulled open.

"What's goin' on out there?" came a gruff voice from inside the hotel.

Clint couldn't see much more than a shape in the darkness, so he made his best guess as to where the other person's eyes were and spoke in that direction. "We need a room. Are there any available?"

There was some more grumbling and the squeak of a lantern's knob being turned. As the flame grew, it illuminated the face of a grizzled old man. Another half twist and the fact that the old man was wearing only long underwear became plain to see.

After looking Clint and Rachel over quickly, the old man said, "I got rooms, but if yer lookin' for a bed to take that dance hall girl and do your business with her, then there's rooms for that in the saloon where you found her."

Clint suppressed a smile when he felt Rachel tense as though she might reach out and slap the old man.

"I beg your pardon?" she said roughly. "I'll have you know that—"

"We just want to sleep," Clint interrupted. "Not stand here and be insulted."

The old man thought for a moment and then stepped aside so he could pull the door open all the way. He started walking toward a battered desk, lighting another few lanterns along the way. When he got behind the desk, he turned and shrugged at Rachel.

"My apologies, ma'am," he said. "But with all the trouble goin' on tonight, I wasn't in the mood for more of the trash that gets attracted to that damn saloon or that damn racetrack."

"That's fine, I guess," Rachel said grudgingly.

"What about that racetrack?" Clint asked. "I've heard about it, but haven't seen much of it."

"Then you must not've been lookin' too hard. It's just south of town, plain as the nose on yer face. By the way, I'll need you to pay for one of the rooms in advance."

"We only need one room," Clint replied.

"Well, you say you don't want to use my hotel for a brothel and I don't see no rings on yer fingers, so I figure you must need two rooms."

"All right," Clint said, not wanting to argue anymore. He put some money on the counter and said, "Will this let us get somewhere to sleep or do I need to find somewhere else just to keep from bickering all night?"

"This'll cover you fer both rooms," the old man said as he turned and plucked two keys from where they hung on the wall behind him. "You need anything else, just let me know. Me or the missus will be right here during the sensible hours of the day."

Either there was no register to sign or the old man was too tired to dig it out because as soon as he had his money and had handed over the keys, the innkeeper only told them which rooms they had before wandering off. Clint followed the bobbing light of the lantern as the old man headed toward the narrow staircase and went up. From there, it was a simple matter of finding their rooms and opening the door before the old man's light disappeared into his own room.

Clint's and Rachel's rooms were across the hall from one another, which reminded Clint of when she'd been knocking on the wrong door to find him earlier that night. There was a lantern on the table next to the door and when Clint lit it, he was surprised at what his money had bought. The room was comfortable and a decent size, making him wonder if Rachel was just as pleased with her own accommodations.

For the moment, all Clint was concerned about was the bed. It was a large four-poster and it barely creaked when he sat down on it after dropping his saddlebags onto the floor. He tossed his hat onto a nearby chair, laid back and closed his eyes.

The comfortable silence lasted only a few minutes before he heard a soft rapping on his door. After what he'd seen and heard of the old man, Clint was fairly certain it wasn't him knocking just loud enough to be heard.

He got up, answered the door and let Rachel inside. "We could get in trouble if we get caught in the same room, you know," he chided.

"Let him come," Rachel said as she moved forward and wrapped her arms around Clint's neck.

He barely managed to shut his door before his hands became glued to her body. At that moment, she felt so good in his arms that he didn't want to let her go. Her lips were soft and warm. Her kisses rained down on his face as she pressed her breasts against him.

Clint moved her over to the bed and lowered her onto the blankets. "We really should be quiet if we want to stay here," he said.

"Then I guess you'll have to undress me real slow."

He did just that and soon, their naked bodies were writhing, entwined in the near darkness. Every so often, a suppressed moan would drift out from the back of Rachel's throat.

THIRTY-TWO

Even after all that had happened the night before as well as the vigorous activity that had taken place in his new room, Clint managed to get himself up just before dawn. The fact of the matter was that his nerves were still on edge and his mind was racing a mile a minute, despite Rachel's admirable attempts to relax him.

She had moved back into her own room less than five minutes before Clint heard the old man's shuffling feet and grumbling voice come down the hall to let them know when breakfast was served. Judging by the way the old man looked around the room, Clint figured he was there more to make sure there was only one person in there than to announce a meal.

Pleased at what he saw, the old man spoke his piece and went his way. Breakfast was a hearty serving of biscuits, gravy, bacon and coffee and was served by the old man's wife, who was much more the social type.

His belly full, Clint told Rachel to stay put and left to see to the business that had brought him into town to begin with.

* * *

The day turned out to be a cloudy one. Like a reflection of the grim silence that hung over the town, the clouds rolled in to obscure the sun and stayed there. The faces that Clint had passed on his way to where he was going were few and far between; the expressions on them troubled and just as gloomy as the sky.

Clint noticed them only from afar because he traveled by any backstreet or alley he could find. He didn't have to go back to the Desert Spring to know that Wescott had visited the hotel. Part of him wondered if the businessman had bothered going inside or if he'd just burned the whole place down.

If Wescott was more of a fighting man, Clint might have thought the latter choice was more likely. But the man was no fighter. That was why he hired gunmen in bulk rather than by their skill. Whether he got the message Clint had sent or not, Wescott had gone to that hotel.

If he had any doubt of that at all, it was dispelled when Clint walked past the southernmost limit of town and spotted the racetrack that was close to completion. Just as the old innkeeper had said, the place was plain as the nose on anyone's face. It was bigger than anything the Grand Bates Raceway could ever hope to be and there was a small crowd gathered in the middle of the open ground that would be the track.

Those men weren't workers. They were probably all the men Brad Wescott could afford to hire. Each of them was armed and in the middle of the group stood the great businessman himself. Only after Clint walked into the open did Wescott step out from behind his rows of hired guns. But he didn't step too far away from them before placing both hands on his hips and waiting for Clint to close the distance.

"You came," Clint said, walking up to within ten yards of the nearest gunman and coming to a stop. "I wasn't sure if you would or if you'd just try to send some more of your dogs out in your place."

"Of course I came. That's what you proposed in the note you left for me back at your hotel, isn't it?"

"It sure was." Clint took his time and spoke slowly so his words carried across all the empty space. He also took the time to look carefully around at the racetrack for any trace of riflemen lurking in the distance. He couldn't spot any right away, but he knew they could still be there either in the skeletal beginnings of the stands or in the large frame structure that looked to be the start of a stable. Stacked around that building was enough lumber to build two large structures: namely Wescott's stable and Jack's stands.

As for the men he could see, Clint counted seven gunmen right around Wescott and three or four more spread out a little farther away on the track.

"We could have sat down and discussed things in a more comfortable location," Wescott said. "We businessmen don't make our deals outside like farmers or ranchers."

"Speak for yourself, Wescott. I'm not a businessman. I'm just the one that you tried several times to put underground."

Wescott smiled and glanced over to the men behind him as though he wanted to make sure they were all still there. "Some of my men got a little overzealous. That wouldn't have happened if you would have talked things over with me in a civilized manner."

"I was more than willing to talk, but you didn't want to let me catch my breath before trying to put the fear into me. Or did that fella in the Winner's Circle come at me because he was overzealous, too?"

At that, Wescott only shrugged.

"After all that's happened since I've been here, you're lucky I still want to talk," Clint said.

"I only talk business with businessmen."

"Just because you keep throwing that word around doesn't make you a businessman. You're a blackmailer, a thief and a gang boss. Jack Bates is a businessman."

When he heard that name, Wescott cringed as though he'd tasted something rancid. "Your friend Jack Bates is the thief, Mr. Adams. He stole my idea for building a racetrack and even took away some of my own laborers to build the damn thing."

"What does it matter if both of your towns has a racetrack?" Clint asked. "Every town has a saloon and you don't see the owners of those places going to war with each other."

"You don't? Then you must not be looking too hard. One racetrack in this area is a novelty. It's something special. Special enough to draw attention, customers and maybe even a railroad line before too long. Two racetracks within a two-day ride from each other just split the profits. They both become commonplace and to make ends meet, each one has to outdo the other."

"So you just decide to make sure there are no others."

"That's right, Mr. Adams. You have a head for business after all. Now what is it you wanted to discuss that's so important. Make it interesting. My time is money."

"I want all the wood back that you took from Jack Bates and for you to let him build whatever he wants. Let him and his partner be and don't send any of your mutts here within a stone's throw of that racetrack."

If Clint didn't know better, he could have sworn that Wescott bared fangs when he smiled.

"My word," Wescott said. "That *is* interesting. And what if I happen to refuse?"

"Well, since I figure you must have the law around here in your pocket already, I'll have to take it upon myself to work something out on my own."

"The wood's already been put to use," Wescott said,

motioning toward the nearly completed stable and seats. "Just look around you."

Clint returned the other man's smile. He put enough of an edge to it to make Wescott's wolflike visage seem like a pup in comparison. "You've got a lot of men on your payroll. Put them to honest work and get that wood back for me. I'll wait."

For the first time since Clint had met him, Brad Wescott lost his controlled demeanor. His smile disappeared and his fists clenched at his side. "You'll be waiting a long time, you arrogant son of a bitch. Just because you've got a gunman's reputation, you think you can come into my town and talk to me like that?"

"I don't know about the reputation, but yes, I think I can talk to you like that."

"Well, I'll tell you what, Mr. Adams. I will set aside some of that wood you want so badly, make a coffin and bury you in it. Right next to her." When he said that last part, Wescott snapped his fingers.

One of his men stepped forward and tossed someone out into the open for Clint to see.

THIRTY-THREE

It was Laura.

Although most of his common sense told him that Brad Wescott wouldn't be open to reason, there was a slim part of Clint's mind that hoped things could be talked out. If there had been some kind of personal agenda between the two men that needed to be repaired or some other underlying reason for the animosity between Jack and Wescott, Clint could have been the peacemaker.

But there was no hidden agenda. There was nothing between the two apart from the friction that came from a hard head butting against a stone wall. Wescott wanted things his way and had been getting them like that for too long to think otherwise.

Clint saw that now, but he had to give it one last try. At least he'd arranged for the discussion to take place in the open, where he could see what he was up against. Since he was on Wescott's turf, Clint figured that was the best he could hope for.

Now, with Laura on the ground and several guns pointed at her, the negotiations had changed.

"Laura, what the hell are you doing here?" Clint asked.

She somehow looked scared and embarrassed at the

same time. "Jack was doing so well with the talking that he took over with the builders in no time, so I came to see if I could help you."

"And she will help you, Mr. Adams," Wescott interrupted. "She'll keep you from making a big mistake that could lead to a bad end for the both of you."

Clint looked back at Wescott, who was now looking so smug and pleased with himself that he was about to burst. "So what do you want now?"

"I just want you to leave so Jack Bates and I can work through our differences on our own."

"You mean so you can roll over him using all these hired guns? I don't think so."

"Fine," Wescott said with a shrug. "Neither one of you means anything to me." Turning to look at his men, he said, "Shoot them both."

The instant Clint heard that first word come out of Wescott's mouth, he prepared himself for the worst. He was even more ahead of the game because he'd been prepared for the worst from the moment he'd stepped out of his hotel room that morning.

The first to draw was the gunman closest to Laura. He pulled a pistol from his holster even though he cradled a rifle in the crook of his left arm. Before his finger managed to touch his trigger, there was a crack of gunfire and his entire right side exploded in burning pain. His hand lost the strength to hold his gun and he let the pistol fall to the ground.

After that, all hell broke loose.

The next set of shots came from the group around Wescott as the businessman ducked and tried to move himself toward the back of the crowd. Clint could feel the panic in the air like a thick, clammy fog and knew that he couldn't have been more right about the experience level of the gunmen.

Not only wasn't there a seasoned gunfighter among

them, many of the hired men looked uncomfortable just firing their weapons at something that was firing back. Once the first shot had gone off, it sent a ripple through everyone else that caused them to twitch on their triggers before they could take real aim.

Lead was flying through the air in a burning hailstorm, but most of it was wild and none of it hit anything but dirt and wood. Clint lowered himself to one knee and shifted to the side so he presented the smallest target possible. The moment he was in position, he picked out another target and squeezed his trigger.

Another of the men close to Laura snapped back like a puppet on a string and blood exploded from the back of his leg. He twisted around on a knee that had been blown into powder and dropped to the dirt while letting out a pained scream.

The first wave of gunfire had passed and the inexperienced men were finally wrapping their minds around the fact that they were in a real fight. Clint knew that would happen, just as it happened whenever someone's life was put on the line.

That was the time when they chose among life's most basic decisions: fight or run.

Clint figured he only had a matter of seconds before the wild gunfire was turned more in his direction. That estimate was cut down even more when the first rifle shot sounded from somewhere in the distance and a bullet whipped less than a few inches past his head.

"Maybe," Clint thought as he rolled to one side, "meeting at the racetrack wasn't such a great idea after all."

THIRTY-FOUR

Just when Clint was starting to doubt his choice of locations, the next barrage of gunfire erupted like a train that had burst from a tunnel. The explosions popped in front of him and smoke rolled forward in a wave of gritty black. Although there was more lead flying around than there were insects, none of it hit any part of Clint's body and most of it was aimed at the spot he'd been before rolling away from the rifle shot.

In any enclosed space, even the most inexperienced gunman would have hit him by now. Clint figured the open air and wide open area was the main factor in seeing him through this far without a scratch.

Rather than rest comfortably on the incompetence of Wescott's hired help, Clint took a moment to look closely at the area around him. He needed to spot where that rifle shot had come from. With more distance between the shooter and target, whoever had that rifle was less inclined to panic. Also, the sniper was taking more time to aim, which didn't bode well for Clint remaining unscathed.

As if responding to Clint's thoughts, there was a crack of rifle fire in the distance and another round whipped through the screen of black smoke. Even though the chaos was growing with every passing second, that rifle fire was getting closer.

The round hissed toward Clint and came so close to hitting him that he could hear the piece of lead as it passed him by.

There weren't many places to hide on the racetrack and that most recent shot had narrowed down Clint's focus. Whoever had the rifle was near the stable. Knowing that did him some bit of good, but there was still one problem. There wasn't a chance in hell Clint's Colt could send a bullet all the way from where he was to hit anything by that stable.

All of that rushed through his mind in a matter of seconds and when he realized what he had to do, the smoke was clearing enough to make the rest of the gunmen a genuine threat.

"There he is!" one of the shooters yelled.

With that, the men shifted their aim and prepared to let off another volley.

Clint got both feet beneath him and started running in the direction that should have been the last place anyone would have expected. Rather than head for cover or put more distance between himself and the gunmen, Clint ran straight for them, firing a round at the group as he went.

Clint's shot cut a path through the thinning smoke and punched a hole through the forehead of the closest gunman. That man was jerked off his feet and tossed to the earth as though he'd been kicked in the chest by a bull. Blood sprayed from the back of his head and hung in the air like a crimson cloud, sending another ripple of terrified panic through the crowd.

By the time the other men got themselves to look away from the fallen man, Clint was already among them. So far, the gunmen hadn't broken ranks and even had the presence of mind to close in once they saw their target was so near.

The first thing Clint wanted to do was find out where Laura had gone. Once the shooting had started in earnest, he'd lost track of her through the smoke and encroaching number of hired guns. Now that he was inside the group, he could see that Laura was being dragged away by Wescott himself. The only thing that kept them both from leaving the battle was the furious struggle she was giving to Wescott as he tried to move her.

Another rifle shot cracked in the distance. The sniper was getting a better feel for the lay of the land because Clint could feel the bullet nip at his heels as it punched a hole into the ground just behind his left boot. But there wasn't anything for him to do about that now. He'd committed himself to his present course and now he had to see it through.

All this time, the gunshots had been blasting through the air, making the empty racetrack feel more like a battlefield. Clint hadn't heard every single shot, however, and had blocked out most of them so he wouldn't be deafened by the constant roar.

Clint's mind was set on only one thing at the moment and that was what was gripped in the hands of the man closest to him. Ignoring the confusion, the shouting, the gunfire and constant movement, Clint dropped his Colt back into its holster and wrapped both hands around the Winchester rifle that was being brought around to bear on him.

The man holding the Winchester was scowling, certain he was about to be the one to drop the Gunsmith with a point-blank shot. That confident scowl changed immediately to a grimace of shock when he felt his weapon being yanked away from him a split second before he could pull the trigger.

Clint took hold of the rifle with one hand wrapped around the barrel and another gripping near the stock and trigger. Rather than shift it so he could aim and pull the trigger, he tightened his current grip and sent the wooden end of the rifle into the face of the man he'd taken it from.

The stock pounded against the other man's teeth with a jarring crunch, sending him staggering back as blood poured from his mouth. Without missing a beat, Clint swung the rifle in a sideways arc, driving the end of the barrel into the closest torso he could find. The steel slammed against another of the gunmen, impacting with so much force against his solar plexus that he keeled over and dropped into an unconscious bundle on the ground.

One of the men directly to Clint's right took a shot from the weapon in his hands. Although his aim was so far off that he managed only to clip one of his own partners, the weapon he fired was a shotgun and its blast was enough to stagger Clint back as his ears erupted with a piercing shriek.

Clint stood in the middle of the crowd of gunmen. There were more of them either dead or wounded at his feet than there were up and shooting, but the ringing in his ears was enough to keep him from hearing anything else. Not only that, but he was disoriented enough to feel his balance wavering as well.

He had enough presence of mind to see that the man who'd just fired still had one more barrel loaded and ready in his shotgun. With him standing close enough to see the whites of the shotgunner's eyes, Clint knew that he didn't stand much of a chance.

There was nobody standing between him and the shotgun anymore, and already the other man's finger was tightening around the trigger.

THIRTY-FIVE

Clint didn't have time to think. There was only time to act, which was exactly what he did.

Twisting his upper body around, Clint tightened his grip on the Winchester's barrel and allowed his torso to twist back around in the other direction. At the apex of his turn, he let go of the stock and snapped his other arm outward, unleashing the Winchester like the business end of a bullwhip.

The rifle sailed outward like a steel-tipped snake's tongue and smashed against the shotgun as well as the hands that wielded it. Metal and wood met flesh and bone in a powerful impact as Clint's opponent's shotgun let out a powerful roar.

The blast rocked through Clint's ears, but the barrel had been diverted enough so that the lead sailed through empty air before burrowing into another part of the racetrack. Clint didn't waste another moment before swinging the rifle back around in another arc that was a bit higher than the previous one.

Clint had to give the guy credit. The shotgunner actually tried to duck as the stock of the Winchester came swinging his way. He tried, but that didn't mean he was quick enough to succeed.

Rather than cracking him across the jaw as Clint had planned, the stock of the rifle Clint swung like a club smashed into the shotgunner's temple instead and put his lights out quicker than wet fingers on a lit candle. There was a crack of wood against bone, a grunt that Clint couldn't hear through the ringing in his ears and then the impact of the shotgunner's back against the dirt.

That only left one man standing, which was the previous owner of the Winchester now in Clint's hands. Clint finished the job he'd started on that one by sending another jab into the man's gut which put him down for a good, long while.

Clint then flipped the Winchester so he could hold it properly. From there, he levered in a round and took a shot toward the stable. He didn't expect to hit anything, but knew he would provoke the necessary response.

That response came in the form of another shot from the sniper. The bullet hissed through the air and tore a gouge from the side of Clint's left arm that ran from his wrist all the way up to his elbow. If the bullet had gone any deeper, it might have torn up a good deal of his arm. As it was, the bullet sliced through his skin, but didn't make it as deep as the bone. It hurt like a bastard, but it wasn't anything Clint couldn't handle.

The reason that response was necessary was because Clint was looking for the plume of smoke from the sniper's gun. Against the dark backdrop of the stable, that puff of smoke wasn't too hard for Clint to find.

Lifting the Winchester to his shoulder and forcing himself not to think of the pain shooting through his left arm, Clint aimed at the puff of smoke and then raised the barrel just a bit before pulling the trigger. The Winchester barked one time and bucked against Clint's shoulder. He didn't wait to see if he hit anything and instead levered another round into the chamber, aimed and fired.

Clint repeated that process one more time before turning his back on the stable and searching for the two people who'd gotten away from the main body of the fight. He didn't have any trouble whatsoever in spotting Wescott and the woman he dragged behind him since they were both running across an open field.

That was another reason why Clint had chosen to meet there. He didn't have to scout the place out in advance to know that it would be empty of bystanders and wide open.

"Wescott!" Clint shouted. "Let the woman go and stop where you are or I'll drop you where you stand."

Wescott stopped trying to drag Laura any farther, but didn't let her go. Instead, he turned around to face Clint and held out his free hand to show that it was empty. "I'm unarmed, Mr. Adams, but that doesn't mean I can't hurt you. Perhaps you've noticed a few extra shots coming from the distance. Like any good gambler, I didn't exactly put all my cards where you could see them. So, toss those guns down and maybe we can talk this through in a civilized manner."

Those words rolled through the air which had suddenly become very still. Some of the gunshots still lingered in the air, but that could have just been the ringing echoing inside of Clint's head. His hearing was clearing up, but that was mostly due to some fierce effort on his part.

Clint stared at Wescott over the barrel of the Winchester. While stepping forward, he looked over both the businessman and the woman he was holding. Wescott's left hand was wrapped around Laura's wrist and although she was on the brink of tears, she didn't appear to be hurt.

There was a gun belt around Wescott's waist, but the holster was still full. Once again, the businessman proved that he was by no means a fighter and certainly was a liar. It told Clint a hell of a lot more than that, but he wasn't much in the mood for a prolonged conversation.

"Placing some cards where they can't be seen?" Clint repeated. "That sounds more like a cheat than a gambler to me. And as far as those shots from the distance are concerned, I wouldn't be so sure about those anymore if I were you."

Wescott looked at Clint in a way that reminded him of a dog that had heard a train whistle. Clint allowed himself to laugh at the curious tilt to the businessman's head and then he hooked his thumb back toward the stable.

Clint had heard the pained grunt coming from that direction partially thanks to the clearing of his ears and partially thanks to the direction of the wind. When Wescott looked in that direction for himself, he was just in time to see his sniper take a staggering step out and then fall over.

After that, Wescott was more than happy to drop his weapon and release Laura just as he'd been instructed.

THIRTY-SIX

"I may be mistaken," Clint said in a mocking tone of voice. "But didn't you have more men than these when this whole mess started?" He looked around for effect and then shrugged. "I guess you get what you pay for, huh, Wescott?"

Wescott, Clint and Laura were walking away from the track and heading toward the town. Now that the smoke had cleared, Clint felt more comfortable discussing more important matters.

"Where are we going?" Wescott asked.

Clint didn't have the Winchester pointed at the businessman, but still had the weapon cradled in his arm. "I think I remember a nice restaurant a bit farther down the street. It's a little run-down, but places like that usually have the best food."

Judging by the look on Wescott's face, one might have thought that he'd been offered a freshly laid cow pie for his afternoon meal. "I can suggest someplace more suitable."

"I'll bet. Don't worry, though. I don't have much to say, so we can do it at the place I'm headed."

There wasn't much more conversation after that. All

three of them walked down the street like a small group of friends that had a minor dispute to settle. Laura tried a few times to engage Clint in conversation, but she was put off by a sideways look from him that told her he wasn't feeling sociable just then.

The restaurant Clint led them to was a small place he'd spotted when leaving his hotel earlier in the day. Being in one of the older sections of town, the outside of the building was dirty and the structure was crooked, but that was only when compared to the places Wescott himself had paid for.

In fact, the older section of town put Clint more at ease. It was almost like a more lived-in home that wasn't as neat as it could be, but a man didn't feel bad putting his feet up and relaxing. Wescott, on the other hand, insisted on acting as though he was being forced to walk into an outhouse. The distasteful scowl on the businessman's face only made Clint prod him more.

Along the way and even as they walked into the restaurant, Clint had been getting plenty of curious glances from passing locals. They'd been bustling about closer to the racetrack, but quieted down when they'd spotted the three walking away from the pile of bodies left out in the open. Not all of those bodies were dead, but the gunshots that had roared through the air previously was making everyone think the worst.

By the time some of the locals had worked up the nerve to go and see what happened at the racetrack for themselves, some of the men Clint had put down were shaking it off and struggling to their feet. That was about the same time that Clint, Laura and Brad Wescott were finding their way to a table inside the modest little restaurant Clint had chosen.

Just the sight of Wescott was enough to make the server inside the restaurant nervous. Seeing who was with him made the server seem even more agitated; he didn't stay around the table any longer than was necessary. Clint figured that was because of the tension emanating from Wescott; the businessman was the only one at the table who seemed openly hostile.

Laura was acting a bit rattled and a little confused while Clint was the most relaxed he'd been all day. Compared to being the only target in a shooting gallery, breaking bread with the enemy was just another midday meal.

"So what now, Mr. Adams?" Wescott asked after the server had dropped tin cups of water in front of each of them. "If you don't mind, I'd prefer to spend as little time in here as possible."

Clint took a sip of water and shrugged. "Oh, I don't mind one bit. I just need the wood and tools you stole from Jack Bates and your guarantee that he'll be free to run his own business any way he sees fit."

"He stole that idea from me."

"And he says you stole the idea from him. Right now, since you're the one that's been so intent on burning things down and shooting at me as well as those around me, I'm not all that inclined to believe you. Besides, I haven't seen anything that was stolen from you, so you tell me. How does that make you look when compared to Jack Bates?"

Wescott leaned back, looked around and let out a disgusted sigh directed toward everything and everyone he saw. "Jack bragged about fighting back against me."

"I'll bet plenty of people around here have entertained that very same thought."

"Everyone talks big, Mr. Adams. Especially when they're talking about someone better off than they are. Surely, you must know how it feels to have smaller people constantly trying to chip off pieces of what you've built?"

"I hear a lot of hot air coming from a lot of mouths, if that's what you mean. I think the difference is when that hot air starts burning people nearby." Leaning forward, Clint locked eyes with Wescott and spoke in a steady, intense tone. "When people start getting hurt, that's when I feel the duty to step in and start turning off the steam one way or another."

"We're not so different, you know. I could use a man like y—"

"We are very different, Mr. Wescott," Clint interrupted. "Take this meeting for example. My guess is that there would have been gunmen waiting to burn me down no matter where we met. At my meeting here, the only thing burning is the food.

I'm a firm believer in giving people chances. You had plenty of them to show your true colors and I wound up getting attacked after every last one of them. So that means you're out of chances, Brad. Save your fancy talk and threats. All I want is the wood and tools you stole from Jack Bates. I won't even ask for your guarantee about not sending out any more gunmen because I wouldn't even believe you if you gave it.

"Oh, and one more thing," Clint added. "How about an apology to Laura here? You know, for taking her hostage and everything."

Wescott shifted his eyes to look at her. "You have my apologies, ma'am," he said without hesitation.

"Good. Now eat up, Mr. Wescott. Since I didn't see many stacks of lumber lying around that racetrack, I'd say you have some work to do in getting your men together to pull down some of those buildings." Clint took another sip of his water and gave Wescott a smile. "And just to show you I'm a fair man, I don't need the exact lumber you stole. Just tear down one of those buildings and stack it neatly onto some wagons. That ought to do it."

THIRTY-SEVEN

Clint's instincts about the food at the restaurant he'd chosen were dead on. The little place in the older section of town served one hell of a meal and that was even when the owners and workers were trying to rush them out of there. For that reason, Clint and Laura went back to that same place for dinner that evening.

This time, the reception they got was completely different. All it took was the absence of Brad Wescott. The moment they walked in the door, Clint and Laura were greeted warmly by the very same server that had rushed them before. Along with their meal, they got sincere apologies for the previous meal and nobody there would accept a cent to pay for the food.

"After what you've done, Mr. Adams, none of us could see our way clear to taking any of your money," the owner of the restaurant said when Clint had insisted on paying for the meal.

Still holding the money in his hand, Clint replied, "If you're talking about before, I don't blame you for wanting us out of here as soon as—"

The owner, a stout man in his late fifties, raised both hands and stopped Clint in midsentence. "That's not what

I mean. I was talking about what you did for us since you've been in town. What you did for all of us who aren't on that bastard Wescott's payroll."

After taking a moment, Clint nodded and put his money away. "If you insist."

"I do insist, Mr. Adams. This town wasn't always called Wescott, you know."

"Really? How long has this place been here?"

"Going on thirty years now. It started as a trading post and a place to stop before heading into the desert or on to California. I won't bore you with a history lesson, but we were here before Wescott came in and started throwing around his money and siccing his men on anyone who spoke up against him."

"So what was this town called before all of that?" Clint asked.

The owner puffed out his chest and stood up straight as though he was about to salute. "Everton," he said proudly. "It was Everton before and it's still Everton to those of us who don't kiss Brad Wescott's ass."

Clint smiled at that. "Well, maybe Wescott won't find this place to his liking anymore after all that's happened."

"Again, Mr. Adams, that's all thanks to you."

Clint shook the owner's hand for what seemed like the hundredth time and returned the waves that were coming at him from all sides. All this time, Laura hadn't said much and Clint hadn't wanted to push her. When they stepped out into the night air, however, he walked slowly by her side and held her hand comfortingly.

"So how are you doing?" he asked.

Laura shrugged her shoulders and swung their hands back and forth. "I don't know. Tired, I guess."

"Well, you've been through a lot. You made the ride from Driver's Town in pretty good time and then got here to be put at gunpoint. That's a rough day by anyone's standards."

Shaking her head, she told him, "Maybe I feel foolish for coming all the way out here just to wind up being another problem for you to solve. Lord knows you've got your plate full already."

"I'm used to surprises. My life wouldn't be quite right without hitting a hitch like that every now and then."

They were walking toward Clint's hotel. The night was calm. The wind was cool and only blew enough to rustle them like a set of familiar fingers tussling their hair. Overhead, the stars were like a mess of crystals that had been spilled onto a blanket of black velvet.

Even after what had happened, Clint couldn't help but be calmed by the simple wonders of the clear night sky. Thinking ahead to what was still to come, he savored that feeling for all it was worth.

Clint walked along, holding Laura's hand as though he was thinking about nothing more than the beautiful night. There was plenty more on his mind, but he didn't want to let too much of that show until the time was right.

As they walked up to the front door of his hotel, Clint opened the door and let her walk ahead. In the light that spilled out from the inside of the hotel, Clint looked down at the hand he was holding until Laura walked ahead and broke their hold on each other.

"At least you came in at a decent hour this time," the innkeeper said. "Just because you paid in advance, don't think that I'll keep my door unlocked any later than usual. Dangerous types around here, you know."

"Yeah," Clint said as he followed Laura inside. "I know."

•

THIRTY-EIGHT

Clint put Laura in his room and left her there while he went to take care of some more business. He'd had trouble getting Laura past the innkeeper, who predictably had his mind set on getting her a room of her own. Some fast-talking had bought him some time, but Clint knew he would probably wind up paying for yet another room in that same hotel.

Once Laura was squared away for the night, Clint left the hotel and went straight to the Winner's Circle. After what had happened the last time he was there, he felt that going there again might be a mistake. But since Wescott's supply of men was severely depleted for the time being, Clint figured that it was better to go back then instead of waiting for those gunmen to get back on their feet.

As it was before, the saloon was full of drinkers and alive with bawdy music as well as the raucous shouting of the dancers. Clint walked in and went straight to the bar.

"You've got a lot of nerve coming in here," the bartender said. Those words, however, were spoken without any malice and were accompanied by a glass of beer.

Clint took the glass and sipped from the foamy top. "Has Mr. Wescott been asking for me?"

The bartender smirked and said, "Cursing your name is more like it. From the way he's been going on today, you'd think he was the one that won that fight today." Leaning forward and lowering his voice slightly, he added, "But we know how it really went. Anyone with eyes in their heads knows."

Clint took another drink from his glass. He'd been noticing the looks that he'd been getting from most everyone in the place. Although he didn't receive outright pats on the back, the gratitude was plain enough to see in the eyes that were turned his way.

Suddenly, he felt something touching his ribs on both sides. The sensation traveled around his torso and onto his stomach. He didn't have to look down to know that someone was reaching around from behind to run their hands over his body. He also didn't have to look to know whose hands they were.

"I was just about to ask for you, Rachel," Clint said.

The blonde came around, but kept her hands on him the entire time. "How'd you know it was me?" she asked.

"Because I may be a little more popular in this town than I was before, but I don't think everyone would say hello quite that way." He turned around and opened his arms so she could melt against him. The truth of the matter was that he could still remember her touch if he even started to think about the last time they'd been in that saloon.

"You don't know how hard it was for me to keep my distance after everything I heard today," she told him. "I've even heard that you were wounded or dead."

Clint held out his left arm and showed her the gouge which could be seen emerging from his sleeve and running down to his wrist. "I got a scratch or two, but it's nothing serious. Besides, who told you I was hurt so bad?"

She looked embarrassed and said, "That doesn't matter."

"Yeah, well, I think you need to hang around some different card tables."

"So does this mean I can see you tonight?"

"I'm thinking so. I probably won't be in town much longer, so if you'd like to join me for a drink I could set aside some time."

"Is that so? Well, what if I had something else in mind?" Her fingers traced a line down his chest and over his stomach. "Like possibly some dessert?"

Clint smirked and nodded, trying not to appear as anxious as she was making him feel. "That sounds like one of the best offers I've heard all night."

"Excuse me," came a voice from behind them. The voice was somewhat familiar, but didn't strike a chord until the speaker stepped forward, out of the milling crowd.

The man who'd spoken to them was the fat gunman who'd tried to take a swing at Clint the night before in a spot no more than a few feet from where Clint and Rachel were standing. As soon as Clint spotted the fat man's face, his eyes narrowed and his muscles tensed for whatever was on its way.

If the fat man was trying to sound tough before, he dropped the act and shrunk back like a wilting flower. His eyes widened and he held his hands up as if to defend himself. The bruises from his last run-in with Clint looked like dirty smudges on his blubbery canvas.

"I don't want no trouble, Mr. Adams," the fat man said. "I just came to deliver a message from Mr. Wescott."

Clint's hand drifted down toward his gun. He didn't touch the Colt, but he came close enough to make his point. "I believe that's what you were doing last time."

"Y . . . yeah, but this is different."

"Then say what you want to say and leave us be."

"M . . . Mister Wescott wants to let you know that your wagons will be loaded up tomorrow afternoon."

"Really? That was quick."

"I don't know about all that. I just know he wanted me to tell you that."

"Good." Clint watched the other man for a second or two without saying a word. Finally, he said, "You can go."

The fat man only seemed too happy to oblige and scuttled back toward Wescott's table.

"The sooner I get out of here the better," Clint said.

Rachel pressed against him a little more and moved her lips up to his ear so her breath washed over him when she spoke. "I was just thinking the same thing. How about we go somewhere for that dessert?"

"I changed my mind," Clint replied. When he saw the look of surprise and disappointment on Rachel's face, he winked and added, "I think that is the best offer I've heard all night."

She swatted him on the arm and pulled him out of the saloon.

THIRTY-NINE

To be honest, Clint never thought he would spend so much time in the town of Wescott. He knew he wouldn't be welcome by the power structure there and had a pretty good notion that he would have a hard time getting back what had been taken from Jack Bates. After being right on those matters, he figured being wrong on one of them wasn't so bad. Especially when much of that time was spent so close to Rachel Cleary.

He woke up early, as usual, the next day and only woke Rachel up to let her know where he was going. She gave him a kiss, rolled over and went back to sleep. Stepping out of the room, Clint walked across the hall and in a matter of seconds had reached his destination.

The room he'd slept in when he'd first arrived at the hotel was still in his name and even though he hadn't been in it for some time, he knew it wouldn't be empty.

Clint unlocked the door and walked inside. Sure enough, Laura was lying on the bed. She wore nothing but the shirt from the day before and was stretched out on top of the blankets. When she heard him walk in, she rolled over to face him and sat up. Thick curtains were drawn tightly over the windows, keeping out all but a trickle of sunlight.

"You never showed up last night," she said. "I was starting to worry about you."

Clint walked over to the bed and unbuckled his gun belt. After setting the holster down, he lowered himself to sit next to Laura. "I had some things to tend to and after your ordeal yesterday, I thought I'd just let you sleep."

She crawled over the bed and came up behind him. "Well, I'm all rested up now," Laura whispered, her hands wandering over his shoulders and onto his chest. "And I'm very glad you're here."

Leaning his head back, Clint savored the feel of Laura's hands upon him. Her fingertips pressed against him, massaging and teasing him at the same time as she started pulling open his shirt. He could feel her lips against his ear and the tickle of her hair against his neck.

"So what did you do last night while I was gone?" Clint asked.

Laura pulled his shirt open and peeled it off of him completely. Once she'd tossed the shirt aside, she crawled around and lowered herself onto his lap. As she slid her legs around him, she showed Clint that she wasn't wearing any panties beneath the shirt that was bulky enough to be a nightgown. "I thought about what I wanted to do to you when you came back. I've been thinking about it ever since you left."

"Have you?"

She nodded, keeping her eyes locked onto him as though she wanted to devour him right then and there. Her hands moved lower over his body. "Yes. I couldn't think of anything else until I fell asleep. And then, when I woke up during the night and you still weren't here, I

started to wonder if I could even wait for you to come
back to me."

The sound of Laura's voice was having an effect on
Clint and with her hands where they were at that particular
moment, she could tell the moment he was aroused. Clint
shifted slightly to help her as she began tugging his pants
open and down off of him. When she couldn't move them
with her hands anymore, she pulled them off using her
feet.

The way she had to wriggle and shift on top of him to
perform the maneuver only made Clint even more aroused.

"You missed me, too," she said quietly after sliding
her hands between his legs. "I can feel it."

Clint had his hands on her hips to keep her from falling
off of him. He now began to massage her buttocks while
slowly moving his hands below her waist. Her legs were
locked securely around him by the time he touched the
warm, moist place between her thighs, and she let out a
breathy moan and spread her legs open wider for him.

Laura's shirt was similar to the one Clint himself wore,
but with only two buttons fastened, the supple curves of
her breasts tempted him from beneath the fabric. Her nipples hardened as he looked at her and his hands worked
in little circles over her pussy and inner thighs.

Clint followed the signals her body was sending him
and he lifted her up a bit so she could center herself over
his rigid penis. From there, she lowered herself down
slowly until she could feel him fitting inside, between her
legs. Already wet enough to accept him, she lowered herself all the way down, taking him completely inside of
her while letting out a contented sigh.

While Laura began to move up and down on his lap,
he pulled open her shirt and caressed her breasts, pinching
her nipples just enough to make her take notice. She liked

the feel of his hands upon her body so much that she put her hands on top of his just to make sure he wouldn't stop what he was doing.

Soon, Laura slid her hands around the back of Clint's neck and held on tightly as she started to ride him a bit quicker. Clint watched as Laura's eyes closed and her face took on a look of intense concentration as she maneuvered her body to bring herself the most pleasure.

Her hips ground forward as she slid down his thick column of flesh, rubbing against him in just the right way to bring a smile to her face. Clint made that smile even brighter as he waited until the last moment before pumping forward and thrusting into her as she was coming down.

After a few minutes, Clint scooted back onto the bed so he could lean back. Laura moved with him perfectly, adjusting herself so she could ride him without breaking her stride. She placed her hands flat against Clint's chest and rocked back and forth, faster and faster until her breath started quickening into an excited rush.

Just when he could feel the muscles tensing in her legs as well as between them, he grabbed onto her and rolled her over. Then he settled on top of her. He thrust into her a few times before getting onto his knees and rising up over her.

She looked up at him with wild eyes and reached out to run her fingernails over his chest. She could only reach for a second, however, before she was overtaken by the pleasure that was coursing through her stronger and stronger by the second.

Running both hands over the inside of her thighs, Clint massaged her while opening her legs all the way. Now he could push as far into her as he could go, pressing his body against her while driving deeply inside. Laura let out a moan while arching her back against the mattress.

What Clint was doing was more than enough to drive her over the edge and her orgasm came in a continuous wave that shook her entire body.

She clawed against the mattress and bucked her hips against him as one orgasm turned into another, and Clint continued to slide all the way inside of her while strongly rubbing her thighs and lower body. Just as she was getting too tired to make another sound, she felt Clint's hands slide underneath her to cup her buttocks and lift her slightly off the bed.

Pulling her toward him while pushing himself forward, Clint drank in the sight of her body splayed out before him as he pumped into her until he could feel his own climax approaching. The motion of Laura's body combined with his own, and it wasn't long before he felt the same pleasure that had broken a sweat on both of their bodies.

One more thrust and he exploded inside of her, holding her body tightly against his own until he was too exhausted to hold on any longer. After lowering her back onto the bed, Clint dropped down beside her and let out one long haggard breath.

"That was worth the wait," Laura said, curling up next to Clint and resting her head on his shoulder. "That was worth everything."

Clint said nothing. He was too tired to do more than smile.

FORTY

Clint was asleep.

Laura knew that because she could feel his chest rising and falling in a slow, steady rhythm and could hear the strong, deep breaths. Over the last hour, she'd managed to slip away from him inch by inch so as not to disturb his slumber. Her body was still tingling slightly from the pleasure he'd given her, but that didn't change what she had to do.

Slowly, carefully, she worked her way to the other side of the bed and gently lowered herself onto the floor. Her bare feet touched down without a sound and she immediately got her bearings in the dark. Her eyes were already adjusted to the shadows, but she wanted to be sure not to knock into anything that might wake Clint up.

She was soon able to maneuver like just another one of the shadows and she padded over to Clint's side of the bed. Her toes bumped against something smooth and cool. She could feel leather as well as the touch of metal against her skin, and she smiled to herself as she bent down to reach for what she'd found.

Her fingers were just feeling along the texture of worn leather when she heard something that made her stop right where she was. Clint was stirring under the covers. His body shifted and turned until he got comfortable in his new position.

Laura was just about to start moving again when she heard something else.

"Looking for this?" Clint asked.

Before she could react to the question, she saw the lantern beside the bed flare to life and the room was flooded with the warm glow of the brightening flame, which added to what little sunlight could make it through the curtains.

Clint twisted the lantern knob only once, not wanting to make it too bright but also wanting to be able to see what she was doing. He'd already had a sneaking suspicion, which was confirmed when he realized that she had been squatting down and reaching for his gun belt on the floor beside the bed.

Laura stood up and smiled at him warmly. Her toes were still touching the belt as well as some of the extra bullets stored there. "I didn't want to wake you up, Clint."

"I'll bet. It would be a whole lot easier to shoot me if my eyes were still closed."

Her smile faded and was replaced by a genuinely hurt expression. "Why would you ever think such a thing?"

He smiled back at her, but the expression on Clint's face wasn't nearly as warm and it wasn't even angry. Instead, he looked more disappointed than anything else. "Well, finding you trying to steal my gun while I was sleeping is a pretty good start."

Leaning down toward Clint, Laura allowed the unbuttoned shirt she wore to fall open. Her firm breasts were accentuated nicely in the warm light, making her skin look the color of lightly creamed coffee. Her nipples were darker and slightly erect after rubbing against the rough material of her shirt.

"I wasn't trying to steal your gun, Clint," she said in

her own defense. "I almost tripped on it when I was coming around to wake you up."

Clint nodded, his expression brightening only slightly. "Ah, so that's the story you're going with? I was expecting more, especially from someone in this as deep as you."

"In what? If you mean this whole mess with Jack and Mr. Wescott, then I sure as hell am in it pretty deep. My life and my livelihood were almost wiped away by that skunk."

"Stop it," Clint said. His voice was so sharp that it caused Laura to recoil. He sat up and swung his feet over the side of the bed. "Just stop it. I'm not in the mood to hear this kind of bullshit anymore."

"I don't know what you're talking about and frankly, Clint, you're scaring me."

Clint didn't have to tell Laura to back away. As soon as he got out of bed, she was already backpedaling from him. She didn't stop until her heels hit the door and at that moment, there was a look of desperate hope flashing in her eyes.

Laura started to reach for the door handle, but was stopped by nothing more than a raised eyebrow from Clint. That was all she needed to see to know that she wouldn't be allowed out of that room. Well, she wouldn't get out without a bit of trouble from an armed man, anyway.

"Are you going to tell me what's going on?" she asked. "Or are you just going to shoot me?"

"It's about you working for Brad Wescott," Clint said.

All the hope and innocence drained out of Laura's face upon hearing that. So, too, did most of the color in her skin.

FORTY-ONE

"You want to step away from that door now?" Clint asked. "Or did you plan on trying to act like a babe in the woods some more?"

Although she still had plenty she could say, she knew that none of it would do her any good at that point in time. So rather than waste her breath, she stepped away from the door and clasped her hands behind her back.

Her eyes were almost tearing up when she looked at him. "Why do you think I would want anything to do with Wescott? He's the one trying to hurt me, remember?"

Clint watched her like a hawk. His eyes were cool and his gun tracked her every movement. "Have a seat."

She stepped over to the chair next to the window and sat down. When she started to reach behind her, she saw Clint start shaking his head. "Can't I open the window?"

"Why? So you can let whoever may be watching this room know what's going on? I don't think so."

She dropped her hands onto her lap and crossed her legs. Only now did she finally pull her shirt closed over herself. "This is ridiculous."

Is it? You're a hell of an actress, I'll give you that much. You're so good that I didn't want to believe what

I was seeing even as I saw it. Let's start with the hotel in Driver's Town. When I left after that first night together, I heard someone walking around inside one of the rooms and shuffling behind one of the doors.

"The sound stopped, but I could tell whoever it was had peeked out at me from behind their door. I got that feeling. You know the one. Where you feel like you're being watched?"

"So?" Laura said. "Someone probably was watching you. I wouldn't put it past Wescott to have spies watching me and Jack."

"Neither would I. In fact, that's what I assumed it was, except for one little thing. There wasn't anyone else staying in that hotel at that time."

"How would you know that?"

"Because I checked the register when I signed in. It's a nervous habit of mine, but every once in a while it pays off."

Laura shrugged. The more Clint spoke, the more uncomfortable she seemed being so scantily dressed. "That doesn't mean much. Someone could have checked in when you weren't looking, you know. You were pretty busy. We both were."

I know. That's why I didn't think too much of it at the time. But then there were other things. For example, when I got here, even the man at the front desk of the Desert Spring knew who I was. Wescott was told about me by someone who described me so well that a stranger could recognize me on sight.

"I like to think I've had a lot of experience with women. Something I've learned is that women tend to notice a lot more about someone's face or details of their appearance than your average man. Men notice things like hair color, whether someone's tall or short, simple things like that. Would that make it so someone could know my face before ever meeting me? I doubt it."

Laura shook her head. "You're a famous man, Clint."

Yes. My deeds are famous. My reputation is famous. My friends are famous. My face isn't quite as famous as all of that. My instincts told me that a woman was the one to describe me to Wescott. Just a hunch, but a damn strong one.

"Not only were you the only woman I'd spent a lot of time with lately, but we also got pretty close. You saw to that, didn't you?"

As she listened, Laura watched Clint with growing discomfort. She shifted in her seat as though the wood was getting hot and she wrung her hands in her lap. Clint watched all of this and took note just as he would sitting across from someone at a poker table.

Her eyes alone were telling him plenty without Laura having to say a word.

"I wanted to believe that you wouldn't do something like stab your partner and me in the back," Clint said. "But then you showed up here in town at just the right time."

"Just the right time?" Laura asked as though she couldn't believe what she was hearing. "I almost got killed!"

But you were just in time to give Brad Wescott a nice little bargaining chip to hold over me. There was no reason for you to come here without letting me know. And there sure as hell wasn't a reason for you to come poking around close enough to those gunmen to get yourself captured.

"Seeing you yesterday made me wonder, but it wasn't until I saw something with my own eyes that it all started coming together. You know what I saw?"

The expression on Laura's face was getting colder and more detached by the second. "No, but I suppose you'll tell me anyway."

"Your arms," Clint said.

FORTY-TWO

"What?"

"Your arms," Clint said. " When Wescott had a hold of you, you put on quite a show of struggling and trying to get away. But you're a strong woman, Laura. I've got the scratches on my back to prove it and that was all in fun. You should have been able to get away from a man Wescott's size.

"Why didn't he have one of his men hold you? That was another question of mine. The only physical thing I've seen him do here is lift his cards and his drink. After the whole scuffle, when I had you to myself, I saw your arms and you know what? They weren't even bruised."

Clint waited a moment for that to sink in. In that time, he watched Laura's face and saw that she seemed more angry than scared anymore. She didn't even seem upset by having the gun pointed at her.

"If you'd put up such a struggle, your arms would have at least been bruised from having Wescott hold on to you. That tells me you weren't truly struggling and the only reason for you not to struggle at that moment was because you were where you wanted to be and doing what you wanted to do."

"So is that why you came in here and had your way with me this morning?" she asked. "To get one more toss before pulling a gun on me?"

"No," Clint said. "I wanted to put you at ease. Isn't that why you let me walk in here and have my way with you?"

She didn't have an answer ready for that one.

Clint went on to tell her, "I also wanted to give you one last chance to prove me wrong because I knew you would probably make your next move against me after getting me all worn out and happy.

"So don't bother looking all offended at my conduct, Laura. The only reason you're so upset is because I managed to beat you at your own game. I told you I've had a lot of experience with women. Not all of them were good girls. Believe it or not, I've also run into bad girls like you. Maybe some that were even worse. But if they only were good for one thing, it was to teach me a lesson."

"Let me guess," Laura said sarcastically. "Don't trust a woman?"

"No. It taught me that a pretty face can hide an evil mind. Men have a tendency to let things slide when they come from a woman, even to the point of not listening to their instincts. I've fallen into that trap before and hell, I may fall into it again. But not this time."

"You're a son of a bitch, Clint Adams. You know that?"

"To people who try to hurt me, my friends or innocent people? Yeah. To people who sneak up on me and try to shoot me while I sleep? You bet I am."

"All I was doing was—"

"Save it, Laura. You've got guts, I'll give you that much. I've seen plenty to show you for what you are and you still try to talk your way out of it."

"Well it's either that or just sit and wait for you to shoot me, right?"

Clint stared her straight in the eyes and let the silence become so thick that she nearly choked on it. Finally, just when the last bit of color had drained from her face, he said, "Wrong." And with that, he lowered the Colt.

She eyed him suspiciously, not sure whether it was safe or not to move or even take too deep a breath. "So what, then?"

"First, I'd like to know why you turned on Jack. Or were you ever really working as his partner?"

"Oh, I was his partner, just like I told you before. Jack let me in on some great arrangements, but then they started to pay out less and less. Soon, they weren't paying at all and then we were losing money. But did that ever stop Jack? Not at all. He just kept sinking both of our money into every little scheme until he was going broke and taking me with him."

Now that she was no longer staring down the barrel of Clint's modified Colt, Laura shifted in her chair to get a little more comfortable. "Then this racetrack idea comes along. I thought it sounded like something that might actually work. The only thing was that I was running out of the money my pa had left me, so if this one went under, I was done for good."

She shifted in her chair and opened her legs just enough for Clint to get a look between them. When she saw that his eyes didn't shift so much as a fraction of an inch, Laura covered herself up again and let out a short, frustrated sigh.

"Brad Wescott came to both of us," she went on to say. "Both me and Jack, first together and then separately. I wasn't interested in what he had to say at first, but when he talked to me alone, the offer was much more tempting."

"You would rather do business with someone like Wescott than Jack?" Clint asked.

"That wasn't it exactly. He just offered me more money if I came in on my own."

"But you had to do more to earn it, didn't you?"

"I sure as hell did. Brad just said we were protecting our investments. You know something? It was worth every dime he paid me."

Raising the Colt slightly, Clint said, "Until now."

She stared at the pistol and was unable to hide the fear that flashed across her face. "Yeah. Until now."

"I've got to tell you, Laura. You're playing a dangerous game. Not only are you putting yourself in a situation that may get you killed, you're putting your trust in the wrong place."

She laughed once in a way that sounded more like a disgusted snort. "Wescott's giving me more money than I ever saw with Jack."

"And you think he'll just pay out all the time and be a good little partner? He's got a history of stabbing his partners in the back. I know that much just from paying attention since I've been here and listening to what you had to say. Whatever you did to seal the deal with him, I doubt it was good enough to keep him from killing you whenever he sees fit."

"I can take care of myself."

"I hope so." Clint stood up and took a few steps back. "You can start now by getting out of here, leaving town and trying to make an honest living somewhere else."

"What?"

"You heard me. Get out of my sight and try to stay alive long enough to make a fresh start somewhere over a bridge you haven't burnt yet."

Laura's face was skeptical and her motions were hesitant as she got up from her chair. "So you're giving me a head start?"

"A head start makes it sound like I'll be coming after you. I don't want to see you again after you leave this room, and I better not catch you trying to crawl back to Jack either."

Clint recognized the sly grin the instant it started to creep onto the corners of Laura's mouth. "And before you start thinking you're too lucky," he told her, "maybe you should wonder what will happen if you go back to Wescott and tell him that the only blood you managed to draw on me was with those sexy scratches I've got on my back. He'll be more apt to kill you than I am."

Clint couldn't say for sure whether or not Wescott would kill her for her failure. What he did know was that Laura's grin had dropped out of sight and she looked more frightened than when he'd had her at gunpoint moments ago.

More than anything, he had too much to do to worry about her any longer. After all, there weren't any trustworthy lawmen Clint could hand her over to even if he wanted to go that route. If he could just get her to leave on her own and possibly rethink the way she was going about her business, then that was good enough for him.

Judging by the way she quickly gathered up her clothes, that was exactly what she was going to do.

"Oh," Clint added. "Leave that gun of yours behind as well."

She started to protest, but dug the derringer out of her left boot and tossed it onto the bed.

That had been a complete guess on Clint's part, but it had paid off. With his luck holding out like that, he figured he might want to visit the card tables at the Winner's Circle before he left.

FORTY-THREE

Clint wasn't happy about the way things had turned out with Laura. If there had been any law in town that didn't belong to Brad Wescott, he might have turned her over to them. Then again, since Laura didn't get the chance to steal from him or to take a shot at him, Clint figured that letting her go was the next best thing.

Although he wasn't a big believer in fate, even Clint had to admit that it had a way of dealing with people in the best ways. Besides that, if women were going to be jailed every time they led a man astray, there wouldn't be enough jail cells open to hold the real criminals.

Keeping his eyes and ears open every step of the way, Clint gathered up his belongings and left the room only a minute or two after Laura had gone. From there, he went across to the room where he'd left Rachel. Last time he'd seen her, the blonde was sleeping, and when he walked into the room, she was still in almost the exact position as before.

"Come on," Clint said. "We need to get out of here."

Rachel rubbed her eyes and reached out to give him a kiss.

Clint took her hand and practically pulled her out of the bed. "No time for that."

"Are you leaving town?"

"Afraid so. I need to wrap things up and move along."

"Are you going to finish off Brad Wescott?"

"In a matter of speaking. Whatever happens, you might want to put some distance between yourself and him. He seems like the type to try and make himself feel better by being rough to anyone who spoke a kind word to me while I was here." Clint dug in his pockets, removed a folded wad of money and handed it over to her.

She looked up at him with a hurt, angry expression. "If you think I'm the kind of girl who was spending time with you for money, then you—"

"I want you to take this and it's got nothing to do with the time we spent together. You might want to leave town after all of this for the reason I was just talking about. However this turns out, you either may not have a job left or it may not be safe for you here. Use this money to see you through whatever rough patch comes along."

"And what if everything's fine?"

"Then buy me a big dinner the next time we meet. Just take the money, Rachel. Please."

She reached out and took the bills from his hand. She kept hold of him and pulled herself closer to him so she could kiss him passionately on the lips. "I expect to see you again, Clint Adams."

"Good. That way when you do it won't be too much of a surprise." He slid his arms around her and when he started to lift her up from the bed, she leapt into his embrace.

They kissed for what seemed like several hours, although it was only more like a few minutes. When they finally broke away from each other, it was very reluctantly.

"Thanks for your help, Rachel," he said, gently setting her onto her feet beside the bed. "It really meant a lot to me."

She waved off his words. "It really wasn't much. You put more flush in my cheeks than I've had in a long time."

Clint thought about poor Jack Bates and his luck with business and women. He then thought about Laura Damon and how her lies had almost gone unnoticed just because Clint, as well as Jack, wanted to give people the benefit of the doubt. "No, Rachel. It does mean a lot. Thank you."

After a few more whispered words of good-bye, Clint led her out of the room and down to the lobby. After making sure his bill was squared away, Clint was about to escort her outside when he was stopped by the gruff voice of the old innkeeper.

"You got a message waitin' here for ya," the innkeeper said.

Clint turned and asked, "Do you know who it's from?"

"Sure do. Brad Wescott."

Clint took the folded message, but before opening it, he asked, "When was this delivered?"

"If you would've come down them steps a minute or two earlier, you could have taken it yourself."

"Thanks." With that, Clint escorted Rachel outside and started walking down the street.

"What's the matter Clint?" she asked him. "What does that note say?"

He still hadn't opened it and instead got them both moving down the street at a quick pace. Only when he'd put some distance between themselves and the hotel did he stop and look at the paper. He didn't even really have to unfold it to know what was written there. Just to be sure, however, he checked it anyway.

Sure enough, the neatly printed words were just as he'd expected.

"My wagons are ready," Clint said. "Looks like Wescott's got no other option than to pay up."

FORTY-FOUR

Leaving the town of Wescott was a quick and painless matter. All Clint needed to do after collecting Eclipse and preparing the stallion for a ride was show up at the spot mentioned in his note and say he was ready to go. Waiting there for him was four wagons full of lumber stacked neatly in the carts. Each wagon even had a driver waiting for Clint to arrive.

"Wait here one moment," Clint said to the closest driver.

Flicking the reins, Clint had Eclipse break into a run and he steered the Darley Arabian toward the other side of town. Sure enough, the stable near Wescott's racetrack wasn't even half of what it used to be. Two of the four walls were gone and those piles of lumber were nowhere to be seen.

Clint had wanted to visit the spot just to be sure that Brad Wescott hadn't pulled one last spiteful act by tearing down some part of the older part of town and stacking it in those wagons. Apparently, the businessman had decided it wasn't worth it to risk Clint's anger just for some petty bit of payback.

At least Wescott had been right about something.

Even though it was well past noon by the time they left, Clint gave the order and led the caravan out of town. It was the time of year where dusk would come sooner rather than later, but it did Clint a world of good just to get away from Wescott and his town.

The moment Clint was far enough away from the place that he couldn't see it no matter which way he turned in his saddle, he felt his shoulders relax and his mood improve. He didn't let himself get too relaxed, however, because he was still involved in the business that had nearly gotten him shot several times over. But it was too late to break off now, even if he'd wanted to.

In for a penny, in for a pound.

That phrase held true now just as well as it had when he'd first agreed to help Jack Bates. Just because the end of his involvement was in sight didn't mean Clint could lower his guard. He was still involved and that could still be enough to put him in jeopardy.

It was well past sundown until Clint finally suggested that they stop and make camp for the night. With the slowest of the wagons setting the pace, it appeared as though the trip back to Driver's Town might take closer to three days. The caravan had made good time considering they were carrying several full loads of lumber, but it seemed to Clint as though grass would grow faster than they were moving.

The hours had dragged by because not only was Clint waiting to deliver the wood he'd gotten, but he was also waiting for the second proverbial shoe to drop when it came to Brad Wescott. Even after all he'd gone through to get the lumber back, Clint felt it had been too easy. He knew there was more to come.

The only question was when it would arrive.

It wasn't until the wagons and horses had all been stowed for the night that the second shoe finally fell. Clint was tending to Eclipse and removing his saddle so he could use it as his pillow for the night when he spotted a shape approaching in the distance.

If it hadn't been for the brightness of the autumn moon, the other shape might have gone unnoticed. Clint narrowed his eyes when he spotted the shape and tried to act as though he didn't notice. Casually, he took the spyglass from his saddlebag and took a look for himself when most of the wagon drivers' backs were turned.

The figure was a solitary man on horseback. Clint watched the rider approach until it closed to within a hundred yards. From there, the rider took something from his saddle and swung his leg over so he could drop effortlessly to the ground. As Clint watched, it seemed as though the figure dropped like a rock through molasses. That was when he could see what the figure was holding.

It was a rifle.

What disturbed Clint even more was the fact that the rifleman practically vanished the moment he hit the ground.

Clint collapsed the spyglass and dropped it into his bag. He backed away from Eclipse and looked around for any trace of other riders approaching from other sides. He saw no more shapes in the moonlight, but he did see plenty in his own campsite to catch his interest.

All four of the drivers were standing clustered around one of the wagons. The moment they saw the serious expression on Clint's face, they pulled aside a false cover that had been made to look like a stack of wood. That particular stack was hollow and had been filled with enough weapons to arm every one of the men Wescott had sent.

FORTY-FIVE

In a strange sort of way, Clint was relieved to see not only that he'd been right about Wescott making one more move against him, but also that the move had finally been made. The only thing worse than a battle was waiting for it. Now, at least Clint could deal with the fight and stop thinking about it so damn much.

The drivers already had their weapons in hand by the time Clint squared off against them. Like four boys reaching into a cookie jar, they froze where they stood and waited to see who would make the first move. Clint had his back to Eclipse, his eyes on the drivers and his hand hovering over his holster.

Every second that ticked by, Clint imagined that rifleman creeping closer and closer to the campsite. For some reason, that single hidden rifleman worried him more than the four armed men that were right in front of him.

"Wescott must be paying you guys a hell of a lot for you to pull this after what happened to the last ones that tried," Clint said. "I'll tell you what. You men can either leave those guns behind and start walking back to town or you can take your chances with me. But I'm warning you, if you choose the latter, I won't be nearly as generous as I am now."

The men glanced at each other and then back to Clint. They saw his hand near his Colt and felt their own hands wrapped snugly around their own weapons. Each of the four drivers looked again, back and forth, before one of them made the decision for all.

That one driver was the man standing farthest away from Clint and he was so eager to take his shot that he squeezed off a round before he'd given himself a chance to aim. That burst of movement and gunfire was enough to spur the others into action and the remaining three brought their guns out from hiding and swung them around to fire at Clint.

The first gunshot was still rolling through the air when the next ones came. Like staccato bursts, the shots rippled through the night, accompanied by flashes of fire that illuminated each of the drivers in turn. All of the drivers had wild desperation in their eyes and pulled their triggers as strongly and quickly as they could.

Clint kept his eyes on the men and dropped to one knee as the shots roared out in front of and around him. He drew the modified Colt and aimed in one fluid motion, pointing the gun as though he was pointing his finger at the closest driver.

Clint squeezed his trigger four times in quick succession. The only parts of him that moved were his eyes, arm and finger as he took his shot and shifted his aim after each bark of the Colt. When he'd taken his fourth shot, every gun in the campsite went silent.

The Colt smoked after delivering its fatal payloads and the rest of the guns were no longer in living hands.

All four of the drivers dropped to the ground like leaves falling from a tree. One or two of them bounced off the wagon as they fell, but every last one wound up in a pile in the dirt. The weapons in their hands could very well have been toys for all the good they did their bearers.

Without missing a beat, Clint lunged toward Eclipse. He sensed the rifle shots before he even heard them and cringed as the bullets whipped through the air an inch or so from his head. He knew the rifleman was good because it was only thanks to Clint's own erratic movements that he didn't catch a piece of hot lead before making it to Eclipse.

Jumping onto the stallion's back without the benefit of a saddle, Clint held on to Eclipse's mane and touched his heels to the Darley Arabian's sides. That was all it took to get the horse moving and both Eclipse and Clint were racing toward the last spot where the rifleman had been sighted.

Clint cursed the sweat that was trickling into his eyes as he searched for any trace of the rifleman's position. The only clue he had was the sighting he'd first made and the direction the last shot had come from. All in all, those things weren't enough to inspire much confidence.

Like a gift from above, the moonlight glinted off of something metal in Clint's line of sight. Seeing that, he threw himself from the saddle and kicked Eclipse in the haunches as he left the horse's back. He didn't like hurting the stallion even a little bit, but that kick turned Eclipse off of his original course a split second before the next rifle shot came.

Clint could feel that he was in the other man's sights even if he couldn't see the rifleman in front of him. Thankfully, the bullet from the unseen gun hissed through the spot where Eclipse would have been if he hadn't been steered away. That way, neither man nor animal were so much as grazed.

Heading toward the ground face first, Clint held his hands out in front of himself and tucked his chin against his chest before hitting the ground. When he landed, he balled himself up and rolled in the sparse weeds surrounding the trail. He stopped himself with an outstretched leg and used the rest of his momentum to bring himself back onto his feet.

The moment he got his bearings, Clint spotted some movement not too far from where he stood. Once again, he saw the glint of moonlight off a rifle and his instincts took over from there. He twisted at the waist to squeeze off a shot from the Colt, which sparked against the side of the rifle that had been sailing through the air.

Seeing the way the rifle turned when it was hit and the way it toppled end-over-end onto the ground, Clint knew the weapon had been thrown as a distraction to draw his fire.

Since the rifleman was unarmed, yet still damn good at keeping out of sight, Clint looked around for the one thing he knew he wouldn't be able to hide so well: the man's horse.

Clint knew where Eclipse was, so when he spotted the other horse less than ten yards away, he knew that was the horse that had brought the rifleman out to the campsite. Keeping that horse in sight while glancing around, Clint readied himself for an attack from any side.

He only had one shot left in his pistol and no time to reload, which meant his life could very well be riding on that single shot.

"Whatever Wescott's paying you," Clint said to the wind since he still couldn't see the rifleman, "it's not enough. You're obviously smarter than these other hired guns, so think about where you are now. I've got what I want. Let this matter drop, and you can walk away."

For a moment, there was no sound to be heard. Even the wind had stopped blowing as if out of respect to the gravity of Clint's situation. Then, suddenly, there was the sound of something rustling against the weeds followed by a glint of metal directly in front of Clint and slightly to the right.

The other man was so good that he had almost made it to his horse without Clint noticing. Like a plume of smoke rising up from a campfire, the rifleman stood up from where he'd been hiding and took aim at Clint with a .45 caliber revolver.

Clint barely had enough time to think when he spotted the other man. Luckily, Clint didn't need to think. His body was already reacting, his lightning-quick motions fueled by the pure instinct to survive.

The Colt spat its final round toward the other man, who was still not much more than a wraith holding a gun. Without much else to aim for, Clint's last shot had been fired at the pistol in the dark figure's hand. There was a spark of lead against steel, a snarled curse and then the flash of movement as the other man raced to his horse.

Clint figured the other man was going for another weapon, so he immediately flipped open the Colt and started reloading. What he heard next, however, was not another gun being drawn, but the rumble of hooves as the horse took off in the opposite direction.

After a few moments, Clint was confident that the other man was leaving and not coming back. He searched the area and was able to find the other man's gun which had been damaged in the fight as well as several leaves covered in warm, inky liquid.

The liquid was blood, which only appeared black in the moonlight. Clint could tell by lifting some of it to his nose and sniffing the coppery fluid. Apparently, more than just the pistol had been damaged by Clint's final bullet.

At that point, Clint didn't much care whether the rifleman was mortally wounded or had just gotten a scratch. The dark figure wasn't coming back. That was all that mattered. Clint didn't even care who the rifleman was. He was just glad that Wescott hadn't been smart enough to hire a bunch of men like that one to guard his interests. If he had, things may have turned out differently.

But Clint was too tired to think about what could have been. The important thing was that even though he didn't have drivers, he still had the wagons of lumber and horses to pull them. He could rig something to get the wagons the rest of the way to Driver's Town. Once there, Jack could build his racetrack and take his shot at building a fortune as well. The track may work and it may break his back, but either way, Jack had the right to try.

As soon as Clint dropped off that lumber, his part in the racetrack business was done.

Jack would be better off without a partner anyway.

FORTY-SIX

Brad Wescott sat in his office, impatiently awaiting news from the men he'd sent out to kill Clint Adams. He drummed his fingers against the expensive mahogany desk and mentally added up how much money he'd lost in manpower alone. Losing the racetrack simply wasn't an option. He would rather see all of Driver's Town burn than give Jack Bates the satisfaction of beating him in their little competition.

Just when he was about to check his window for the sixth time in as many minutes, Wescott saw his office door swing open and his most expensive hired gun walk through the door.

"There you are, Galloway," Wescott said with his normal smug grin. "I was wondering if I would have to send out a search party for you."

"My money," the rifleman said. "Where is it?"

"Is Adams dead?"

"No."

Wescott's nostrils flared and he clenched his fists at his sides.

"Then you won't get any money, you stupid piece of sh—"

The businessman's words were cut off by the sharp crack of a gunshot that sounded like the snapping of a whip inside the enclosed space. Wescott staggered back a step and looked down to find the source of the sudden pinching pain in his chest.

He wanted to call for someone to help him, but his heart was no longer beating due to the fresh hole that had been blown through it. Even if he could find his voice, there was no one else left to answer him.

Galloway slid his pistol into his left coat pocket and used that hand to rub the space where his right trigger finger used to be. The wound was fresh and every lick of pain he felt from the bloody stump at the end of his hand made Galloway curse the name of Clint Adams.

Even as he looted Wescott's money belt and office, Galloway figured up how long it would take before he could go after the man who'd taken so much from him with one lucky shot in the dark. All he needed was more practice using his other hand.

When that day finally does come, Galloway swore to himself, *Adams won't know what hit him.*

Watch for

DEAD END PASS

272nd novel in the exciting GUNSMITH series
from Jove

Coming in August!